COMIN' HOME SOON

And

OTHER SHORT STORIES

Volume I

Christmas Carol Kauffman

Compiled by Marcia Kauffman Clark

DIGITAL
LEGEND

Christmas Carol Kauffman

1901–1969

Christmas Carol Kauffman was born on December 25, 1901, in Elkhart, Indiana, the second daughter of Abraham Rohrer and Selena Bell Wade Miller. Carol, as she was known, graduated from Elkhart High School and attended both Hesston and Goshen Colleges. She began writing short stories at Hesston College and continued writing one short story per month for the *Youth's Christian Companion*. In total, she wrote more than one hundred short stories, twenty-two of which are captured in this volume.

In 1929 she married Nelson Edward Kauffman. They served together at the Hannibal Mission Church in Missouri for twenty-two years, where Nelson was the pastor. They are parents of four children. While in Hannibal, Carol began writing book-length inspirational true stories that were published by Herald Press.

Lucy Winchester, her first book, was published in 1945. Throughout the next two decades she authored six additional books: *Light from Heaven* (1948), *Dannie of Cedar Cliffs* (1950), *Not Regina* (1954), *Hidden Rainbow* (1957), *For One Moment* (1960), and *Search to Belong* (1963). After her death, two more books were published in 1971: *Little Pete and Other Stories*, a collection of thirteen of her short stories, originally written in 1928, and *One Boy's Battle*, written in 1948 and originally titled *Unspoken Love*. All nine of her books continue to be published today.

Christmas Carol Kauffman died on January 30, 1969.

For
Nellie Marie Miller Mann Whitmer
Who typed most, if not all,
of Carol's short stories

Send inquiries to:

Digital Legend Publishing

1994 Forest Bend Dr.

Cottonwood Hts., UT 84121

U.S.A.

Visit www.Digitalegend.com/Carol

or write to info@digitalegend.com

or call toll free: 877-222-1960

Printed in the United States of America

ISBN: 978-1-934537-93-0

Version 2 (May 2010)

Interior and cover design by Sutherland Publishing (King City, Oregon)

Contents

Foreword

Christmas Carol Kauffman's reading audience was largely a rural one. Families for the most part didn't have a lot of books, let alone fiction in their homes. But, like people of all generations, they longed for and loved a story with a spiritual message. The stories that were printed in the *Youth's Christian Companion* filled a need in their lives, a need to step out of one's life into another by way of reading a story, particularly a story about someone outside of their day-to-day lives.

The stories you are about to enjoy were creations of Carol's very rich imagination. Many of the characters and circumstances came, not from her personal experience, but from her remarkable imagination. She also had the ability to carry a story along by use of conversation that made the characters more real.

The central theme in these stories can be found in the winning speech she gave at Hesston College, where she spoke about the most important word in the English language—not mother, not love, but the word *come*. *Come* is a word of inclusiveness, a welcoming word, a word promising comfort and companionship. But most of all it offers a way for people to find redemption, to find a new life, freedom from what is troubling them. Carol's characters go from loneliness to inclusion, from darkness to light. Her stories are about people who find redemption. Important words given in that speech at Hesston College became her central theme over many years.

Because of her use of conversation, these were good stories to read aloud or to listen to. Each week our family looked forward to the arrival of the *Youth's Christian Companion,* so we could read the story about Lucy Winchester. I had the privilege of reading the continued story to the rest of the family. We discussed what we thought would happen next, and we were happy or upset with what was transpiring; waiting patiently for the next month's edition.

The main difference between her early stories and the later novels was that the novels were based on real individuals she had met and learned to love while serving in the Hannibal, Missouri Mission Church.

A deep spirituality is evident in each individual story, whether short or long. Each one reflects the central part of Carol's goal. Her life was devoted to bringing people to the light; to have them experience the Savior's redeeming sacrifice individually. Carol understood how a life could be turned around when a person answers the call to come into that light and find love and companionship in the fellowship with the followers of Jesus Christ.

Yet Carol was a very down-to-earth, practical person with a real sense of the enjoyment of life. I lived with her family and helped in the mission at Hannibal. I had the privilege or typing *Not Regina* from her hand-written pages. Christmas Carol radiated joy, a sense of fun, laughter and delight. She had a wonderful sense of humor and always brought out the best in others.

In spite of Carol's continual service as pastor's wife in the mission church, caring for her family and welcoming the many visitors who stopped by (often unannounced), she never gave up her love of writing. Although she had only her bedroom, where she was often interrupted by a member of the household, she also wrote an amazing number of novels. Nine to be exact.

Carol enriched many lives through her writing talent and played a very important role in my life. My memories of her are ones that I will always cherish.

—Esther Stoltzfus Wilson, Vancouver, British Columbia

Preface

Within the Goshen College Historical Library archive files containing Mother's correspondence with Herald Press is a box with copies of the *Youth's Christian Companion*. At the time I was writing her life story, I was aware of this wonderful box, but was so focused on the events of her life that I did not take a peek into what you are about to enjoy. When I finally took time to peruse the magazines, I rediscovered the twenty-one original short stories written by Christmas Carol Kauffman.

Reading these stories anew reminded me that perhaps many of her readers had not enjoyed these precious short stories for perhaps more than sixty years. Mother's novels continue to delight new generations of readers with their poignant portrayals of faith-filled lives. And her short stories are no less touching. Therefore, I am excited to bring you, within the pages of this book, twenty-two of Mother's short stories. Twenty-one were previously published in the *Youth's Christian Companion,* and one is a short story I found while researching her biography. That story, "Comin' Home Soon," was first printed in Mother's biography, *The Carol of Christmas: Life Story of Christmas Carol Kauffman* (Digital Legend, 2008).

It has been forty years since Carol's death on January 30, 1969, and more than eighty years since she, just shy of her twenty-seventh birthday, picked up her pencil and created from her remarkable, creative imagination her first story as an adult woman. But that was not her first story; someday I will share the very first story she wrote as a little girl in grade school.

I always knew Mother was brilliant. She excelled in everything she decided to do with her heart, mind, and hands, especially her writing hand. The only thing she decided was not a necessity was learning to type. That rare experience of typing her short stories became the privilege of Mother's oldest sister, Nellie. Mother would grab a piece of paper, used or new, and in a very short time would imagine a story that immediately grabbed a reader's undivided attention and keep it captive until the very last word. Each story completely different than the previous one, until she had imagined up more than one hundred short stories!

Chapter 19 of *The Carol of Christmas* includes a response Mother wrote in 1954 to the managing editor for the *Youth's Christian Companion:*

"Twenty-seven years ago I received my first letter from Brother C. F. Yake, informing me that a short story, which I had written for a class assignment in literature, while a student at Hesston College, was accepted for publication in the YCC.

"To be sure, I was pleased. But the next line nearly took me off my feet, for it told me I had a talent to write, which should be developed and dedicated to God and to the Church.

"Talent to write? Stories? Me? Surely the letter had been missent. Looking at the envelope once more I began all over. I held my breath, for the concluding paragraph, asked if I would agree to send him a story a month! Something inside me quivered. It unfolded slowly, came alive, grew, and grew from Kansas to Pennsylvania to a place I had visited once as a child.

"From that day to this, Brother Yake has been a friend, a special friend, and a brother, a Church Father of inestimable inspiration to me. He made me feel somehow that we must be workers together in one great printed effort to save our growing people, from the world, for God and the Church. Without such a relationship between editor and contributor, writing stories, at least for me, would have ceased long ago."

On May 20, 1965, the Elkhart Truth newspaper printed mother's response to an interview about her gift in writing: "'I have to know what the last sentence is going to be before I write the first.' Says the Elkhart novelist Christmas Carol Kauffman."

Mother was further quoted in the article: "The prospective character must have been 'someone in emotional conflict' who resolved it with a satisfactory conclusion based on religious faith. The complete work has to tell a 'lesson in life.'" Her primary goal was to glorify God.

Mother wrote many short personal prayers in a small book she shared with me in the early 1960s. One in particular rings true of her inner beliefs: "Because you made me, you understand my ways. Today I am determined to love thee more, trust thee more, and witness for thee in an unusual way. I am very ordinary, but you are extremely extraordinary. Therefore, since I am yours, you can do great things through me."

Mother was an extraordinary woman. She did great things within her tremendous gift of writing. As you read these following short stories you will come to realize that her God-given talent for writing the life stories of others was remarkable in itself, but she was also truly gifted in the ones she dreamed up in her mind, which was full of "one-of-a-kind stories," as she took her lead pencil in her gifted right hand.

I wish to again, express gratitude to my mother, Christmas Carol, for following her heart's desire to inspire us as readers to have a greater determination so serve the Lord more fully. To Dennis Stoesz of the Mennonite Church USA Historical Committee who granted me the privilege of typing these short stories from the *Youth's Christian Companion*'s original pages, and to Joshua Byler, from the Mennonite Publishing House/Publishing Network, for granting me permission to reprint Mother's short stories. Because of this wonderful privilege; you will experience the same rare treat that her initial readers experienced more than eighty years ago.

Much gratitude and appreciation also goes to Boyd J. Tuttle my publisher, who has given me this wonderful opportunity, and to

Anastasia Tyler my editor and designer. Without both of their help you would not hold this priceless gem in your hands.

Special thanks to Esther Stoltzfus Wilson who has graciously agreed to write the forward. I was eight years old when Esther came to live with our family in Hannibal, Missouri. She was like a second big sister, whom I looked up to with fond admiration.

And lastly, I again express appreciation for the blessing of calling Christmas Carol, Mother.

—Marcia Kauffman Clark

Comin' Home Soon

By *Carol Hostetler Kauffman, age 30, March 17, 1932*
Excerpted from the book The Carol of Christmas

Christmas Carol Kauffman never used a typewriter. She always wrote all of her stories in longhand, with a pencil (just as is shown in scanned archival images over the following pages), and mail them to her older sister Nellie to type. Nellie would type the stories and send them back to Carol.

One such story was found in the Goshen archives among the many letters and correspondence relating to Carol's life. It was in an envelope addressed to her parents and dated March 17, 1932. The envelope contained several sheets of folded paper upon which was a handwritten story that Carol must have intended Nellie to type, but for some unknown reason never found its way to Nellie. Subsequently, this wonderful gem never saw the light of day, never was typed, and never was sent to Youth's Christian Companion. How fitting that now, nearly eighty years later, Carol comes to us as fresh and pure as if she wrote only yesterday.

The story is especially poignant when you consider that the heart of the message derives from a letter that also failed to reach its intended recipient, yet the effects of that letter are deeply felt by all those who read it. It is as if God allowed Carol this one last turn at the loom, a moment to weave, in her skillful and simple way, a story that in the course of a few short sentences reaches deep inside even the most calloused heart and there tugs at the strings with a skill and compassion born in the fire of affliction and yet touched by the Master's grace. At the end of this particularly moving story, Carol writes a brief note to Nellie as if dashing off

1

a story like this were an afterthought that she could have, should have, attended to earlier:

Dear Nellie,

I think every time I finish one story, I won't wait so long to begin the next one, and every time I seem to let it go till the last minute. The poem, I copied from a book I have. It is not original. Ma Donna Lee [Carol's oldest daughter] has been cross today. I didn't get her to sleep till one o-clock. I am baking bread and beans now. I wish I could send some over. This has been such a gloomy, rainy day, and such mud, but I am much happier in my heart than I have ever been. One tract you sent helped me most, the story of the sea captain. I say that verse over every day.

To read the rest of the life story of Christmas Carol Kauffman see The Carol of Christmas, published in 2008 by Digital Legend Press.

**

The quartet took their seats. A strange hush like a solemn benediction fell over the church. Even the red and white carnations in the baskets beside the pulpit seemed to drop their heads an instant. The ushers tiptoed to the door to bring in the latecomers. A young man with sandy hair and well-worn shoes and tattered suit, took a seat just inside the door.

The minister rose. "I think it would be fitting after the song to just bow our heads a moment in silent prayer, thanking God for our Christian mothers." The sandy head twitched, then went down with the others.

"We have come here today," said the minister opening his Bible, "to pay tribute to the best friend, the dearest and truest friend you or I have ever known. No human name is so enshrined in humanity's affection like the name of mother. For most of us everything that is beautiful, sweet, lovely and noble, clusters around that name. Think of mother and you think of home. Think of home and you think of the Bible. Think of the Bible and you think of God. And more to the

Comin' Home ~~Soon~~

The quartette took their seats. A strange hush like a solemn benediction fell over the church. Even the red and white carnations in the baskets beside the pulpit seemed to drop their heads an instant. The ushers tiptoed to the door to bring in a few late comers. A young man with sandy hair and well worn shoes and tattered suit took a seat just inside the door.

The minister rose. I think it would be fitting after this song to just bow our heads a moment in silent prayer, thanking God for our Christian mothers. The sandy head twitched then went down with the others.

"We have come here today," said the minister opening his bible, "to pay tribute to the best friend, the dearest and truest friend you or I have ever known. No human name is so enshrined in humanity's affection like the name of mother. For most of us everything that is beautiful, sweet, lovely and noble clusters around that name. Think of mother and you

man whose heart does not respond to the music of the two words, mother and home."

For twenty minutes the minister held his audience. Hardly a child made a whimper. Many a heart beat faster than the ordinary Sundays, but no one saw or knew why one spotted heart jumped madly toward his throat. Often throughout the audience a patch of white went to the eyes.

"And now," concluded the minister, "after another song, Marjory Smith will give a closing number, after which we will rise for the benediction."

A slender girl of about seventeen took her place on the platform. Her voice was clear but shyly sweet.

"There's a feeling comes across me,
Comes across me often now,
And it's the deepest, seems when trouble,
Says its finger on my brow.
Oh, it is a deep, deep feeling,
Neither happiness nor pain.
But a strange and soulful longing
To see mother's face again.
You don't know how much you love her,
That old mother—till you roam way off,
When her voice can't reach you,
And with strangers make your home.
Then you know how big your heart is.
Seems you never loved before,
When you get this soulful longing
Just to see her face once more.
Mother, tender loving soul!
Heaven bless her dear old face.
I'd give half my years remaining
Just to have her one embrace,
Just to shower love, warm kisses
On her lips and cheeks and brow,
And appease this awful longing
That comes so often now.

The audience rose with one accord. The benediction was pronounced, and the young man on the back seat slipped from the room unnoticed.

It was dusk when a call was sent into the city hospital that a young man with an attack of acute appendicitis was found in the north end park, and was being brought in immediately.

An operation was performed at once. Shortly after midnight the young man turned and for the first time spoke to the nurse beside him.

"I'm better, ain't I Miss?"

"Yes, but you are still quite sick." She felt his pulse.

"I, I thought I was goin', once." He choked on the words and stared wildly from feverish eyes.

"We thought so, more than once." She moistened her lips. "But, you must not talk yet."

"But I must, I must. You see I ain't wrote or heard from my parents for 'leven years. Won't you write a note for me?"

He tried to raise a hand, but it remained limp beside him, rough, brown and helpless on the white sheet.

"You'd better wait a few hours. You must not talk now."

"Now, now," he whispered huskily, "please now!"

Without knowing why, the nurse obeyed him. It was her custom to have patients obey her—but something in the man's voice, something in his pleading eyes sent her quickly after paper. She drew up her chair.

"My old cast-off mother," he began.

The girl looked up sharply. "What? You don't mean?"

"Yes, write it, for that is what she is. I cast her off and left her 'leven years ago. Please write. It's 'leven years, now since I run off and left ye, but I took one look at yer face. You, I left and it's followed me all these years, that dear face like when ye told yer little boy to say his prayers." He stopped for breath.

"It always comes before me, in all the bad places I've ever been, an kep' me from goin' clear down. I'm rough now mother an' I've seen lots of trouble an' knocks, but yer face always smiles at me. Sometimes it has tears on the cheeks, an'—"

"Wait a minute sir." Something blinded her that she could not write. Her hand shook. The man did not notice, for his eyes were half-shut.

"I'm in the hospital now, but I'm comin' home, soon as I get well, an' take care of ye. Ye shan't know a care or worry, only be near me with your dear face. This is Mother's Day and I happened into a church. I was so tired. God forgive me and God bless ye, till I come. I'll come home soon, yer wanderin' boy Jack".

The nurse folded the partly blurred sheet and reached for an envelope.

"Why, Jack! Mr. Jack!" She bent over the man. "What's the matter Jack?" She shook him. "Just a minute Jack. Where shall I send it?"

Your mother—your mother!" "Jack, where is she? Jack!" "Oh," she whispered, "may her face be among those that welcome you."

She leaned over the man and something from her lips fell on the sandy hair and calm face. And just then [in] the moon pictured on the wall above him, what seemed a face, a mother's face smiling down on her sleeping boy.

Two Tiny Mighty Persons

By Carol Hostetler, age 26, Hesston College, Hesston, Kansas
Originally published December 2, 1928,
in the Youth's Christian Companion

I t was nearly midnight. All was quiet except for the constant beating, splashing, dripping, draping of the rain on the pavement below. With hands clasped behind him and a wan, troubled face slightly uplifted, David Lee stood staring out upon the silvery gray veil of soft rain. Although the man was but thirty-three, the shoulders, once straight and firm, were now bent and stooped, the hands were a little trembly; the brown hair was mixed with silver; and there was something about the eyes that made one think it took more than overwork to bring. Twenty minutes passed, thirty minutes and still the man stood gazing out upon the night with a look of intense scrutiny. Suddenly he thrust his unsteady hands into his pockets, walked to a desk at the farther end of the room, took out a sheet of paper and began to write.

32 Berrymoor Apartments
Peoria, Illinois

May 5, 1927

My dear Mother,

The evening is past, and a new day is upon us. You wonder why I am up so early? So do I. It is a splendid time of day to think, when all, or most of the world is asleep. I do it often; especially on nights like this.

7

I received your letter two weeks ago, I believe, and am indeed glad to hear your rheumatism is better, and that Marie is so thoughtful of you. Take good care of yourself, Mother.

I do not wish to cause you any worry, Mother, but perhaps I could not cause you anymore than I have in the past ten years. Ten years! Mother, it's been that long since I have known a happy day. Or was I ever happy? I don't know anything tonight, except the heavy consciousness, that I've never been able find those things for which my heart has longed. Yes, I can imagine I can see you press your lips, and give a nod of understanding. You were right, Mother, as you always are, when you told me that night I left home, that I would never find true happiness, unless I gave up to your wish and Stella's. Stella! How that name, and the memories it brings, have followed me to this day. O memory! It chases me, and stares me in the face wherever I go. Tonight I am sunk in dejection and loneliness enough to confess to you, Mother, that I made the biggest mistake of myself that has ever lived, when I refused to take the step that would have brought joy to you, and me, and Stella, perhaps. All these years I have been lying to you, by trying to make you believe I was content in my work, and content to let Stella go, rather than give way to my own pride and selfishness . I have kept my misery and remorse to myself for ten years; but tonight it hangs over me like a dark cloud about to swallow me up, and I feel as somber as the night outside. In the morning, doubtless, I'll feel better, but a night like this is an ideal companion for intense emotions.

Pardon me for referring to Stella again, but I remember how greatly you loved each other. I do not blame you, Mother. She was the very ideal of beautiful womanhood. I have never seen her, or heard of her since that night. I can still see her wistful, pleading, angel face. Oh, if my memory could but fail me!

Get ready to laugh, Mother, when I tell you of one of my new ideas. How about my adopting a couple of children? No, I am not joking. I am too old and gray for that. You know I always did have a large place in my heart for youngsters, and I haven't changed much. I never really thought of doing this until a month ago. A new family moved into the neighborhood with two of the cutest children you ever saw.

The little girl is about three, with flaxen curls clustered about her pink, dimpled baby face. The boy is about eight, he has a crippled leg, poor chap, but such a bright sparkling happy face. Strange how I became acquainted with them; but I pass their home twice a day going to and from the office, and they are always watching for me, and come scampering out to the walk, or call to me from the porch or window. I have never seen the parents. The mother works, and the father sleeps days and works nights, I believe. They have none too much money, but they must be fine people, for the children are so sweet and polite. The little queen's name is Rosalee; and her brother's name is Holly, and they call me "Uncle Man" Can you imagine that, Mother?

No, no. I am not thinking of adopting these children. They have a home, but they have just made me overly interested in youngsters, and I thought that I might visit some institution and perhaps find two children of that type. Maybe I could forget my misery by wrapping my interests in a couple of mischievous little things. You will understand, Mother. Perhaps I could come home with them? This is only a suggestion, and may be an unwise one. Tell me what you think.

I fear this long letter will weary you, but I trust you will write to me soon, and in the meantime, take good care of yourself, Mother. The clock just struck one-thirty.

A loving good-night,
David

David Lee folded the sheets without re-reading them, sealed and addressed the letter, turned out the light and slipped into bed, and fell into a troubled sleep.

The morning dawned bright and warm. Every bird, every budded twig, every soft, spicy breeze seemed to proclaim in trembling ecstasy its joy for the radiant, dazzling springtime.

Holly and Rosalee were playing on the porch of their humble little cottage, when David Lee came down the street on his way to the office. The brilliancy of the morning had banished some of the gloom from his face, and with a smile, he greeted the children as the one came tripping, and the one limping down the path to meet him.

"Me's been up a long time today, Uncle Man," said Rosalee in a little voice that rang out like a silver bell. She clapped her tiny, plump hands with glee. David Lee caught the little bundle of sunshine in his arms and tossed her high above his head.

"I'm glad to see my little girl so happy this morning," he said. "And how are you, Holly?" He held the little cripple close to his side and stroked his sandy hair.

"What have you been doing this morning, Holly?"

"I've been studying my Bible verses," he answered proudly.

"Bible verses?" inquired Mr. Lee with surprise.

"Oh! Didn't I ever tell you 'bout that? Mother has me learn a Bible verse every day an' nen on Saturday night, Mother gives me seven pennies to put in my bank, if I can say seven verses clear thru."

"I can say a verse," said Holly.

"An, jes' little verses she can say," said **Rosalee**.

"I tan say, 'Dod is lobe,' and '"Esus loves 'ittle chilin', an' 'Esus lobes Uncle Man."'"

"Are you sure he does, Rosalee?" asked Mr. Lee earnestly.

"Oh, yes," nodded Rosalee, her flaxen curls bobbed up and down with her head.

"Muver said, '"Esus lobes everybody!' An Muver knos," added Rosalee triumphantly.

"She does?" Uncle Man smiled. "What verse can you say, Holly?"

"'Not my will, but thine be done.' An' yesterday I learned, 'Though your sins be red as apples, God can make them white as snow.'"

"I must go, children," said Mr. Lee apologetically. "Will you each tell me a verse each morning if I give you a penny for your bank?"

"Oh, yes, yes," they shouted. "Muver tan pick out nice ones," Rosalee said assuredly.

With happy hearts the children ran back to the stoop, but the children's friend passed down the street in bewilderment. Like a mountain stream rushing down on the valley below, so thoughts of mother and childhood flooded his sin-sick heart. Bible verses! His mother, too, had once taught him verses to repeat in Sunday school, but that was twenty-five years ago. How happy he was then, like the little children he loved now. How in utter contrast to his present state of circumstances!

The day proved to be a strenuous one, but never for a minute did David Lee forget the Word of God, as given to him that morning from the lips of children. "'Esus lobes Uncle Man" kept ringing in his ears, like the song of an angel. He found himself repeating it over and over with pleasant satisfaction.

The next morning the children were unusually happy, as they earned their pennies with their verses.

"Dod made de heben and de earf," Said **Rosalee** in babish accent. "Heben is where daddy is."

"You have no daddy?" Uncle Man asked with great astonishment.

"Sure, we have a daddy, answered Holly "but he went far away, an' we're going there, too, some day."

"What is your verse, today Holly?"

"Whosoever believeth on the Lord shall be saved."

The children ran to the house to bank their pennies, and again David Lee passed down the street in deep thought.

The ways of God are stranger than the thoughts of man. Very small persons can often in their simple childish ways touch the hearts of those in which angels have despaired. The brightest flowers in all the world are the tiny human blossoms that grow and sing and play around the porch of a Christian home. It is strange that the man, who had spurned so often the Word Of God, was now, after long years of disobedience, being touched by a few words from these little blossoms in God's great garden?

David Lee found himself more anxious every morning for their verses. Often the children ran down the street to meet him, as each day their little hearts grew happier and lighter, David's grew sadder and heavier with the consciousness of sin.

One evening he found among the mail on his table, a letter from Oregon. He tore it open and read:

May 10, 1927

R. R. 4

Salem, Oregon

My dear Son David,

Your letter came as a great surprise to me, but a happy one. Happy to have you be confidential with me, but sad because of your unrest of soul. David, I knew it all the time. I could read between the lines, and I have been praying for you, always.

How well I remember what a dear sweet baby you were, what a cute, manly little chap you were at seven, how bright and promising at twelve. How anxiously I prayed over you at fifteen, and sixteen, and how happy I was when Stella came into your life. I could see at once the influence she had over your life, and David, maybe her sincere devoted life is still inspiring you on to greater things. Thank God for Stella. Perhaps all these years she, too, has been praying for you. You thought she didn't love you because she refused to marry you unless you would be a Christian, David, your thoughts were wrong. She thought you did not love her or you would have been willing to give up your ways.

I do not wish to add to your remorse, but I believe I'll tell you what happened after you left home that night. Stella came over to me and threw her arms around my neck, and cried till she could cry no longer. We talked, and prayed and cried till two o'clock in the morning. She was too tired and exhausted to go home, so I took her to bed with me. The next morning she was very quiet and pale as a sheet. Oh, how could anything so beautiful and rosy and beamy, fade and wilt so over night. Tell me she didn't care, David! I know better!

She stayed at home a month or more, and came over to see me every day. We expected you to return. Stella grew thinner and quieter every day, and one day she came over and kissed me good-bye, and said she was going to Denver to work in the Orphan's Home. I received a few sad letters from her, and all at once they stopped coming. The next fall her parents moved away, and I have never heard from them. You never mentioned Stella's name before, so I never did.

As for adopting children-David- it brought tears to my eyes. Your whole letter did. I believe my eyes are blinded by them now—wait a minute. Wouldn't I be happy, to have you come home with a little girl on your arm? David! I have always loved little girls so, since Mamie died. Remember? I still have her dear little clothes and playthings. But you like boys, don't you? One of each would be nice. You have made me all excited, David, so you dare not disappoint me. You can't come too soon.

The strawberries will soon be ripe, and the mock-orange bushes at the back porch are beginning to bloom, and the walnut tree has branches large enough now to put a swing on. I am washing windows today, but I need someone to move the step ladder for me, and I need a pair of little eyes to watch from the inside, to see that I get all the specks. Come David, a thousand times, yes.

Please read tonight the first and thirteenth Psalms, David.

Your loving Mother

P S- Do not be too hasty in deciding on the children: that is, I mean, find out all you can first of their parents. The influence of good honest parents is so marked.

Mother

David folded the letter slowly, and sat for some time staring intently at the carpet. He would never let his mother know he had no Bible in his room.

Suddenly the man's heart melted, the drawing power of the Spirit of God seized hold of him, and with feelings that words cannot express, his body shook with great sobs. He sank on his knees before the table, and called, and cried unto the Lord, and the Lord heard his voice. A deep sea of calmness and joy flooded the man's soul such as only those who have experienced salvation can appreciate. Going to the phone he lifted the receiver.

"Thirty-nine please."

"Western Union?"

"Telegram please to Mrs. Elizabeth Lee, Salem, Oregon. R. R. 4. 'Saved through the precious blood of Jesus. Joy beyond measure. Taking morning train to Denver. Signed-David.'"

At eight forty-five the following morning, David Lee left his apartment room with a song on his lips.

"Just fifteen minutes to reach the station," he said to himself. "I'd better call a cab. No, I feel like walking this morning. Praise God!— It's good to be alive. And to think I might have been enjoying this happiness all these years, and Stella! Lord, help me find her. If she is not at the Orphan's Home they can tell me when she left there. But I am too anxious. It would be too good to be true; but Lord, may it be too good; as are You."

As he neared the little cottage where Holly and Rosalee lived, he did not see a sign of any children. At first he was disappointed, but on second thought, added, "I don't have time to talk with them this morning anyway. I am going for something better."

At that moment a faint cry was heard from the open door. It was followed by a louder cry, and the pitiful shriek of a little girl. The door burst open and Rosalee came running down the steps.

"Oh, Uncle Man," she choked holding out both hands. "I 'ome fast. Holly falled down, an' hurted hisself an' tant det up, an' his ace is beedding, O," she sobbed.

Grabbing the child to his breast, he bounded into the house. There on the floor under an over-turned chair lay the little boy, his innocent face covered with blood. In an instant David was on his knees beside the limp body, wiping off the blood with a clean handkerchief. He lifted him gently upon the cot in the corner of the room, ripped off his coat and rolled up his sleeves. He rubbed him and called him by name, but the child did not answer.

"O Uncle Man," sobbed Rosalee, "Do Holly hurt?" O Muver, tome home, tome home."

"He will be alright soon, Rosalee," whispered David tenderly. "Holly just bumped his head badly. We must call the doctor."

He did so.

"And hurry. The child is unconscious."

"Rosalee, where is your mother?" he asked.

"Tone to wo'k"

"Where does your mother work?"

"Way down dat way, at de hon fac'ty."

"At Johnston's horn factory?"

"Yes," she wailed, "O tell Muver tome home fast. I huut too."

He went to the phone and called the number.

"O Rosalee, what's your last name? Quick, my dear."

"Rosalee Hamilton. Is Muver there?"

"Johnston's Horn Factory." Came the response.

"Mrs. Hamilton to the phone please."

It seemed fully ten minutes before she came. Finally he heard a delicate, sweet voice say "Hello"

"Mrs. Hamilton?'

"Yes sir."

"You had better come home, Mrs. Hamilton. Your little boy is hurt. I don't know how badly. I just called the doctor. I will stay with—"

"My boy? Holly, you mean?"

"Yes –mam, he fell—"

"Oh!" Was the stifled cry. "No! I'll come at once. Who's speaking?"

But before he could answer she had clicked the receiver.

David went back to the child on the cot, and started bathing his face, while Rosalee hung on his arm.

A quick step was heard on the porch, a muffled cry, and in came Holly's mother.

"O Muver, Uncle Man, he—"

David Lee rose from his knees, turned around, and—

For a moment, silence—the little room seemed to sway in a haze of sweet perfume and cloy eyesight. Then came an ache in the throat, and four eyes grew misty.

"Stella!" David held out both hands.

"David—when, what—O what does it mean?"

"Stella, it means your child has led us."

She rushed to the child on the cot and dropped wearily by its side.

"O my precious Holly, is he dead?"

"No Stella; see the doctor is here now. Do not be alarmed." He placed a strong hand on her trembling shoulder.

"Rosalee, dear, is this Uncle Man you and Holly have told me so much about?"

"Why, yes—yes, I guess so." The color came to her pale cheeks, and the sad eyes grew a little brighter.

The doctor examined the child, and in a few minutes Holly opened his eyes, and looked around wonderingly.

"Mother's here, darling." Her voice quivered a little, and her slender hands were shaking. "Lie still, Holly. Mother will stay here, and Uncle Man is here, too. Did you know he picked you up when you fell Holly?"

With large eyes Holly looked up into his mother's face. Behind hers he caught sight of Uncle Man, holding Rosalee in his arms. He was whispering something to Rosalee.

"Mover"—said Rosalee, patting her mother's face, "Uncle Man said I should say you, he lobes 'Esus too now."

"David, O David." Stella caught his hand and kissed it. In her eyes he caught the longing of his aching heart.

"Uncle Man," said Holly feebly.

"Yes, Holly, what is it?"

"Mother can tell you big, long verses."

"Can she? And she's going to, too."

"Holly," David's voice was almost a whisper. "Look up, Holly. How would you, and Rosalee like to call me Daddy?"

"Daddy?" Holly gave a deep sigh.

That night as the sun was slipping down behind the hills, David's mother was sitting on the veranda, when a messenger boy drove up, and handed her this telegram:

"Coming home on the sixteenth with three sweet children. One is my wife, and two are our children…David"

A Little Word
with a Wonderful Meaning

The Winning Address in a
Declamation Contest at Hesston College

*By Carol Hostetler, age 27, Hesston College, Hesston, Kansas
Originally published January 20, 1929,
in the* Youth's Christian Companion

The English language is comprised of approximately four hundred and fifty thousand words, and in this long list there is one little word of only four letters that I consider the most beautiful, the most appealing, the most powerful and the most full of meaning of any word ever spoken. Now it is the sweetest word to us in America, but also to everyone on the face of the globe, speaking any language. Thousands of people consider "Mother" the most beautiful word we have. Many more have chosen the word "Love" and perhaps you will be surprised when I tell you that above both of these, I place that simple little word "Come—Come." But I would not expect you to agree with me until you have heard my reasons for such a choice.

"COME." The word alone is a beautiful word to say. It is an invitation, an entreaty to draw nigh or move hither, and is full of warm feeling. It excites immediate attention, stimulates action, and is full of the sense of purpose. Come is an invitation to fellowship or companionship, to participate in joy, to receive comfort or relief from distress, and it is often the answer to the heart of longing. It is an invitation to the gate of service, and an appeal of welcome into an abundant life.

The first words I remember hearing were, "Come to Mother." How sweet an invitation! How full of love and tenderness! The first words the majority of children say are,

"Tome det me, tome itt me up." Even a little child selects the word that contains the greatest appeal.

We can all recall the times when father went to town and promised to bring some candy for us on his return. How eagerly we watched at the window, smashing our noses against the hard pane, or sat on the steps of the porch betting with our brothers and sisters that, "The next person will be father, or I'll eat two blades of grass." When finally the most welcome person we ever saw came into view, we ran to the door and gave mother the news, "Daddy's coming." Then we ran down the walk to meet him. And the little mother, taking the fresh bread from the oven, smiled gently too, because John was coming home. Oh, what a tremendous volume of joy and satisfaction is found in that little word "come!"

You are all familiar with that noted painting, "The Doctor." In the foreground a beautiful child lies sick. A kind handsome-looking doctor is anxiously bending forward watching, what is apparently the crisis of the disease. In the background shadow, are the agonizing father and mother. The artist has tried to put in the doctor's face and pose all that is noblest and best in his profession. And as I stand and look at the picture, I can imagine the intense agony of the faces of the parents, change to relief and peace as the doctor looks up and says, "She's going to be all right." Oh, what a tremendous volume of comfort in that simple little word "come!"

In times of distress and suffering, it is as welcome as it is, as simple to say, "Come." Men have been appalled in shipwrecks, men have been trapped in mine explosions, women and children have been caught in fire and flood, when all at once, out of the terrible screams of panic, comes the message, "They are coming to save us," like an answer to prayer.

Tonight behind the bars of the State Penitentiary at Canyon City, sits a man who accidentally killed his brother-in law in a fist fight. For eight years he has been shut in from all the pleasures that you and I enjoy. Several years ago, though the preaching of Gospel missionaries, the man was converted, and because of his fine character and excellent behavior, the court has agreed to release him, if he can secure pardon from his wife and eighty of his relatives. Each year the man sends out letters of request to these people. "It was an accident. Truly I did not mean to take Henry's life. Won't you make it possible for my release that I can return to my family?" Last year the prisoner received "Yes" for an answer from eighty of his relatives, but he cannot yet be set free, because his own wife refuses to forgive him. Several months ago he sent her one of the most pathetic letters one could imagine. "Dear Emily, even if you do not forgive me, just send me one word, "Come", and I will be free." Day after day and night after night the man prays for that one word to be sent to him, and when he receives it, it will be the sweetest and most precious word in the language to him. Oh, what depth of heartfelt meaning is involved in that one little word "Come."

Five years ago my sister and her fiancé offered their services to Near East Relief. She was accepted, but due to the age regulation for men, he was rejected. Their parting was one of the most touching, and pathetic scenes I have ever witnessed. But one morning twenty-seven months later he received this cable gram: "Alexandria due N.Y. harbor May 10 about noon. Come." Holding the message in his trembling hand, his eyes filling with happy tears, he said, "Come, Come, O sweetest word I have ever heard."

"When she comes home again, a thousand ways
I fashion, to myself, the tenderness
O my glad welcome; I shall tremble, yes
And touch her, as when first in the old days
I touched her girlish hand, nor dared upraise
Mine eyes; such was my faint heart's deep distress."
Oh, what a tremendous volume of love and eager anticipation is found in that little word "Come!"

The poets find a beauty in the wonderful meaning of this word that none other can express. All over the country, men and women cherish their poems and unite their voices in their messages. We can never fully appreciate the depth of such hymns as:

"O, Come all ye Faithful!
"O, Come ye Disconsolate"
"Come Thou Fount of every Blessing"
"Come Holy Spirit, Heavenly Dove"
"Come, O my Soul, in Sacred Lays"
"Come ye Sinners, poor and needy"
"Come Thou Almighty King"

As Wm. S. Pitt stood at the door of the little brown church, his pen wrote the sweetest words his heart could frame: "Oh, come to the Church in the Wildwood."

"How sweet on a clear Sabbath morning
To list to the clear ringing bell,
Its tones so sweetly are calling;
Oh, come to the church in the vale.
Oh, come, come, come, come, come
To the church in the wildwood,
Oh come to the church in the vale.
No spot is so dear to my childhood
As the little brown church in the vale."
What a tremendous volume of sacred feeling is found in that
    simple word "Come!"

But the greatest reason why it is the most wonderful word is because it is the appealing message of the Bible. It is the message for all people, white and black, red and yellow, a message that touches every human heart. God first loved us; then because he loved us, He made a plan of salvation and gave his wonderful invitation, "Come." The Father says, "Come;" the Son says, "Come;" the Holy Spirit says, "Come." The blessed angels echo the message, "Come." "Come unto me all ye that labor and are heavy laden and I will give you rest."

Are you poor? Come and I will make you rich. Are you sick? Come, for I can make you well. Are you sad? Come and I will wipe away your tears. Does everyone hate you? Come for I will love you.

Does no one understand you? Come, for I understand. Do you dread the day of death and judgment? Come and that will be the dawn of life and glory. "Come everyone, young and old, rich and poor, black and white," is the loving invitation of the Savior. "Come" is written all through the Bible. It has brought peace and joy to more hearts than any other word is spoken.

The coming of the Christ child brought tidings of joy to the world that no human tongue can express. For centuries the world had been looking for a king, and at last, when on that night the angels from the realms of glory sang, "The Savior is come," it gave our lips a message we are still singing. What unspeakable gladness in that word "Come."

Christ's daily message while on this earth was "Come." "Suffer the little children to come unto me. Come to me, ye poor and crippled, come and follow me. When he neared the tomb of Lazarus weeping with Mary and Martha, he called with a loud voice, "Lazarus, come forth." To the weeping and heartbroken sisters, that was the sweetest word they had ever heard, and their brother came forth alive. History records hundreds of instances telling us how the word "come" was given as an invitation to comfort and joy.

The word "come" is on the lips of every Christian: "Come, taste of the Lord and see that he is good. I invite you to enjoy the blessings of the Lord also." It is the Christian's daily prayer, "Come to my heart Lord Jesus. Come and fill me with thy holy presence." Sometime to every heart comes the message of the unseen spirit:

"Come unto me; it is the Savior's voice, The Lord of life who bids thy spirit rejoice. O, weary heart with heavy cares oppressed, Come unto me and I will give you rest."

But the second coming of Christ is the sweetest message of all. It will be the greatest event in history, when the Savior King comes through the clouds in all His glory. Precious to every believer are His words, "And if I come again I will receive you unto myself, that where I am, ye may be also." He is coming, coming with an invitation. No message has ever been heard that will be as welcome as the word, "Come ye blessed of my Father, inherit the kingdom prepared for you from the foundation of the world. Come, thou faithful servant, enter into the joy of thy Lord." No one can think of a more welcome, appealing, and soul-stirring invitation than that. Oh, what a tremendous volume of reward and bliss is found in that wonderful little word "Come!" Even so come, Lord Jesus.

Her Mother's Son

By Carol Hostetler, age 27, Hesston College, Hesston, Kansas
Originally published February 10, 17, and 24, 1929,
in the Youth's Christian Companion

A tear trickled down the face of the girl as she was setting the kitchen table for two. She took the corner of her blue gingham apron and wiped it away, but when her glance met the ever-understanding, ever-anxious one from the eyes of her mother's picture on the clock shelf, the girl leaned hard against the wall and cried out in pitiful broken sobs.

"Oh Mother—Mother dear!" The girl clasped the picture to her breast. "For your sake, I'll never give up. God will answer our prayers someday—someday mother. I'll die praying for Matt. He can't ever forget you, mother—no."

The sleet outside was beginning to turn into beautiful fluffy flakes. Before long the earth, the shrubbery and every catchable thing was covered with a blanket of white. Men and women were hurrying home from their places of business, news boys were calling out the evening paper, and the bell in St. Monica's Church steeple rang for six o'clock prayer.

In the kitchen of the scantly furnished three bedroom apartment stood Emily Dune preparing the supper on a little oil-stove. She always fixed things that were easily kept and warmed over, because she never knew when Matt would come home.

Since Mother died Matt had gone from bad to worse, and Emily's heart had grown from sadness to the utter depression of grief. Matt was twenty when their mother had her last heart attack. Emily was alone with her when it happened, and her last whispering words were, "Emily, br—bring Matt."

"I will, Mother," sobbed Emily, "but don't leave us—I will—Mother speak—my God, my God!"

Half an hour later Matt came stumbling in half drunk, his clothes wet, and his shoes sopping.

"Oh, Matt, why didn't you come straight home tonight just for once. Matt, Mother is—is dead!"

That experience made an impression on Matt which lasted only two weeks. After selling most of the household goods to pay for the funeral expenses, the two orphans moved into the three room apartment and every night when Emily came home from the printing office, she built the fire, prepared a meal, and waited, and waited. It was the same experience tonight.

The girl bathed her face at the sink and smoothed back her auburn hair. She sat by the window for some time and watched the long purple shadows deepening to black. Crossing the room, she took from the clock shelf, a small worn Bible of her mother's. It opened up at a page where a pressed red rose had been placed, and her eyes fell on a verse that had been underlined with red. "The eternal God is thy refuge and underneath are the everlasting arms." A faint smile lit up her wan, troubled face, and lifting it toward heaven she prayed,

"Eternal God, I rest my soul in your—"

The door burst open and Matt covered with heavy, wet snow, sank, without removing cap or coat, into the nearest chair.

"Well, is the grub ready to eat, kid?" he bawled out in guttural, drunken glib.

"Yes Matt," answered Emily softly. "It's been ready at least an hour."

She took his cap off tenderly like one would remove the hood from a sleeping baby, then stooping to unlace his soppy shoes.

"None of that, old kid." He drew his feet away and raised his drooping head. "You think you're goina' to keep me in tonight, eh? Got the supper on the table? I'm hungry."

"Yes, Matt—I—but—come over by the stove, Matt. You'll catch your death of cold."

"Cold nothin,' Got hot coffee? The boys are comin' 'long at eight o'clock an' what time it now, Sis? I can't see that—eh—this light is so dim."

"Matt, the light is all right. It's your eyes—you've been drinking again. Its ten minutes till—"

"Ten minutes till eight?" He fairly yelled the words at her. "Get the stuff on the table, hot or cold!"

"Yes Matt, it will be ready as soon as you are washed."

He rose to go to the sink, staggered and caught his balance by the open cupboard door.

"I'd rather you stay in tonight, Matt." Her voice was pensive and wistful. "I want to talk to you Matt."

She placed the potatoes and meat on the table wearily.

"Don't start in like that again, Sis," he growled. "I know what you're up to again. Some more of that Church stuff—baby talk— mush—mother's little boy. I'm sick of it!"

His eyes glared wildly and his fists clenched tightly. He came close to Emily, till she could feel his hot insulting breath in her pale frightened face. He had never spoken like this to her before. A strange fear seized her.

"If you ever say another word to me about my affairs, Emily Dune, I'll leave this house and never come back, and you can eat your supper when you sweet please, and I'll eat mine when I please. There's the gang now, and I haven't had a bite to eat just because of your everlasting whining."

"But, Matt dear, I—"

"Shut up, will you?"

"But I was going to say—"

"I don't want to hear what you were goina say!"

Great tears fell from the girl's eyes into the cup of coffee she was holding in her trembling hand.

"Here, Matt, drink this, please. I didn't mean to insult nor boss you. I am only trying to help you because I—I love you—because Mother—"

She could not finish her sentence, but sobbing aloud she pointed to their mother's picture on the shelf.

For a moment Matt stared at the picture, then at his sister and just then the boys outside whistled.

He started for the door and instantly Emily was at his side with her arm around his dirty neck.

"Oh, Matt—Matt—, I can't see you go. Oh, Matt, won't you stop drinking and stop running with that gang? Won't you, Matt? Oh, won't you answer your mother's prayers, and give your heart to God, Matt?"

An infernal laugh shook his body. He jerked off her slender arm and opened the door. The snow on the ground was several inches thick and long icicles hung from the telegraph wires.

"I'm goin' sis." He looked at her with a cruel, glassy stare. "I'm goin', and never comin' back, do you hear? I'm goin to live my life as I please and you can live yours in Church and prayer meetings if you please. Your friends don't suit me and mine don't suit you, so we'll just part for good. I'm goin' in the morning to—"

With that he slammed the door.

Emily stood with a cup of coffee still in her hand; stood paralyzed and dazed.

"Matt going—never coming back—never? Eternal God—everlasting arms—"

The room grew dark, the clock stopped ticking, the air pressed in and Emily fell with a heavy thud upon the floor, her face buried in broken pieces of the heavy hot cup.

How long she lay there, no one knows, but those everlasting arms must have reached down and lifted her up, out from the pool of blood. She reeled and tottered to the door of the adjoining apartment. She somehow made her way to the phone and called the doctor. When he came, Emily was only half conscious and she never remembered being taken to his office, never remembered having stitches taken in an ugly cross-shaped gash on her right cheek.

**

Two weeks passed and Matt did not come back. Several days later Emily was seen leaving the house carrying a brown, battered traveling bag; on her right cheek was a patch of gauze.

A window in the flat above was raised and an old woman thrust her head out curiously.

"Where ye be goin', Miss Dune, honey?"

"I'm—I'm going away for a while, Mrs. Littletown. I can't stand it since Matt left. I've sub rented the rooms."

"I sure hate to see you go child. I'll miss them Church songs ye sang so pretty 'fore ye got hurt, and them Sunday-school papers ye always brung me. Ye look mighty peaked too. Goin' to relation?"

"Good-bye, Mrs. Littletown." The girl's voice faltered. "I'll miss you too." Something in her throat almost choked her.

"God bless you and keep you. I'll mail the papers to you. And if Matt should—should come back, tell him I—love him, and he will find me and our Eternal God by the signs of the crosses."

"What ye mean honey?"

Without answering, Emily followed the icy walk toward town. The old woman stayed by the open window until her friend, the dearest, God had ever sent her, was out of sight.

"Tell Matt—"the old woman almost hissed as she poked the fire in the old coal stove. If I ever see Matt Dune again I'll tell him a-plenty, so I will. How can that beautiful lily, love that low down rascal?"

One stormy night three weeks later, Matt with sleeves rolled up and a butcher's apron on, was making hamburger sandwiches in the window of a dingy little lunchroom on a busy side street in Flint. His face was sunken and haggard, and his eyes were bloodshot. He seemed to be having a good time, however, talking and laughing with the man beside him who was cutting pie and pouring coffee for the long line of customers on the other side of the counter.

An old woman clad in a long, black coat, a rustic old-fashioned bonnet, and a closely woven black veil, stopped in front of the lunchroom and stood close to the window as if to find shelter from the piercing wind. She stood for some time watching Matt flop the meat cakes on the greasy iron. Finally she opened her purse and counted her change, hesitated a moment, and went in. She took a table in the farthest corner of the room and ordered a sandwich and a cup of coffee.

"The sandwich without mustard, if you please sir." Her voice was hesitant and a little trembly.

"One plain, Matt," laughed the waiter. "For your grandmother over there in the corner."

Matt answered with a louder laugh, and tossed the sandwich over the counter. The old woman had her back turned and he did not see. She ate slowly as if she needed to sit and rest, and when she went out the door, Matt thought he heard her give a low moan. He slapped the next meat cake on the iron while he cleared his throat emphatically. He didn't ever want to think of it again, but that moan reminded him of the way his mother moaned the first time she found out that he smoked.

"I hope she never comes in here again," he cursed under his breath. "This is no place for the feeble minded to eat. After Matt left the lunch room that night, he crossed the street and went into a pool room. After an hour he came out dragging his tired feet beneath him. He was breathing heavily. Taking a step forward awkwardly, he all but knocked over the same old woman he had seen in the lunch room that evening.

"I beg your pardon," she said in a low breathy tone. Matt only grunted and trudged on.

The next evening while Matt was frying the meat cakes in the window, he noticed the black veiled woman again, only this time she looked more bent and more hideous.

"I hate her," he said to himself." "The very sight of her gives me the creeps!"

"I saw your old grandmother this morning, Matt," said the waiter a few days later, "down on twenty-first street, wheeling a baby cart for one of them wealthy folks. I sure wouldn't let that old woman take care of a kid o' mine."

"Just so she stays there, is all I care," answered Matt angrily. "And if you call her my grandmother again, I'll finish up on you."

At that very moment the door opened and in stepped that queer figure. The men laughed and sneered and no one offered to wait on her. She stood with one hand on the latch, her other hand holding a small white package. She hesitated, turned to go, then as if compelled, walked over toward Matt, laid the small package down on the counter in front of him and went out. With a whistle, Matt tossed the package across the room to one of the men.

"Here's your birthday present, Jim. Look out, it might be poison."

Jim tore open the paper with a yell of delight, thrust something yellow into his pocket, read something that was printed on a small white slip and tore it into bits.

In an instant, Matt had hold of Jim. "Give me that, you fool!" He had Jim by the throat, and held him thus, while he reached into his pocket and pulled out a crumpled ten dollar bill.

"Is this all of it?"

"All of it, you brute!"

"And what was on that white slip you tore up? Tell me! What!"

Jim did not answer. Grabbing his cap he walked out and did not return. Matt stood gazed and bewildered. An almost terrified expression crossed his face.

He left the lunch room that evening at ten o'clock. The snow was falling gently, covering the icy walks with a thin blanket. He lit a cigarette and was crossing the street when his foot slipped and he fell directly in front of an approaching coal truck. The driver slammed on the brakes, his truck skidded, a woman screamed, and the motionless bleeding body of Matthew Dune lay under the truck.

People ran, people jammed, women screamed, policemen ordered and no one knew who it was that dashed into the nearest store, grabbed a phone and called an ambulance.

It was just driving away from the scene with Matt, when an old woman in a long black coat, a queer rustic bonnet, draped with a veil, darted to a man standing at the edge of the crowd, took him frantically by the arm and demanded, "Have you a car handy, sir?" The man jumped back as if struck. He nodded.

"Get into it quickly." Her voice was strong and commanding. Without knowing why, the man walked quickly to his car and got in. The woman leaped into the front seat beside him. The man turned to her in dumb amazement.

"Follow that ambulance," she commanded, pointing a thin gloved hand to the slowly moving gray cab in the near distance, "I must get there. I will pay you."

**

From her pocket, she drew out a dollar bill and handed it to him. He was too astonished to take it. She thrust it into his coat pocket. Her breath came short and fast. She leaned forward in the seat and watched the gray car ahead of them like a tamer watches the eyes of a tiger. Twice, her body shook compulsively, and she said something in an overtone a driver could not understand.

It was an hour before the door of the operating room opened and the sleeping man, under the long white cover, was wheeled slowly to a room at the end of the second floor, and placed in bed. And by special permission, after much hesitation, the woman who had followed Matt there was allowed to sit in the corner of the room, while the nurse stayed by his bed.

It was after one, when one of Matt's hands moved nervously and he made a faint moan. Instantly the old woman in the corner of the room stood up, made a faint cry as of relief, then dropped on her knees by the window.

In the very stillest part of the night, when every living creature seems to be asleep, and every moving object motionless, and the darkness is its darkest, and the diamonds in the snow under the street lights sparkle, and dance fairy-like, Matt opened his eyes, looked straight into the face of the nurse, felt the pain in his legs and his head, and knew where he was. He KNEW where he was.

The realization of everything past and present stood before him like a map. He could follow distinctly the road he had taken from the time his mother had first whipped him, to the moment he fell in the street several hours ago. Then it hovered over him in a boiling, foaming, tangled mass; it came down around him; it strangled, choked, smothered, and buried him. It grew red, purple, black, thick black. It was killing him. He saw as in a dream, his mother and Emily with radiant faces, not aware of his condition, not trying to help him. Then he saw Emily as she stood with the cup of coffee in her hand, her auburn hair falling in pretty waves around her sweet face, her blue gingham apron, the table set for two, Emily's eyes. In a flash, Matt lived again every action and word of that night.

"Oh, Matt, won't you answer mother's prayers and give your heart to God?" Those words cut him now like a knife. With a shriek the man cried out, "My God, I will," and smote his trembling hand to his breast. The nurse jumped as though struck and caught the man's hand.

"You are—"

"Listen nurse." His voice was begging, but faint and unsteady. "Send a telegram at once to Miss Emily Dune in Marksville, please"

"And what will it be?"

"Come. Go at once please. Oh—Emily, God help her—Emily. Go—go. I am all right—Jesus!"

The nurse left the room. Out of the shadowy corner of the room, rose the old woman who had sunken there in a half-faint. Slowly she measured her way, inch by inch across the room. Silently she slipped up beside the bed and stood there watching the face of the man whose eyes were closed.

A pitiful cry shook his big body and he opened his eyes and saw again the hideous black-veiled figure.

"What—what are you doing here?" His voice was husky and trembling. "Are you a ghost or—or what do you want of me?

I never harmed you. I—I—the money—I am dreaming."

The old woman took hold of the veil and slowly lifted it up over her rustic bonnet.

"No—no—God, my God. Emily—my sister—no. What is that on your cheek?"

He closed his eyes and covered his face with his hand. A terrible, stifled sob shook his entire body.

"My—cross—Matt, do not let it frighten you. I know it makes me look ugly. That's why I wear a veil—and—'"

"But Emily, oh, dear, how did it happen—when?"

"It's alright, Matt. Just after you left—I—you know I had a cup in my hand."

"No—no—, Emily." Great tears came into Matt's eyes and he cried as few men ever do. He caught her hands and pulled her face down to his own and kissed and cross-shaped scar over and over again.

"Are you the woman I made fun of in the lunch room? And are you the woman I refused to wait on this morning, and you are the one the fellows called my grandmother, and you're that angel who brought me that ten dollar bill this morning to spend on drink and cigarettes—my sister?"

"Not for a drink, Matt. Didn't you read what was on the white slip?"

"I didn't see the slip."

"Why, Matt, I'm sure I put it in."

"What was on it, Emily?"

"It's all right now, Matt. I saw you needed a new coat."

She had removed her own long black coat now, and the old-fashioned bonnet, and stood by the bed, the Emily of two months ago, tall, slender, beautiful, her auburn hair falling in soft waves around her sweet sad face; but not the same Emily, for her eyes were sunken and dark, her cheeks were colorless and—the scar!"

"Oh, Emily, I—you—you."

Matt could not talk. He could only clasp her hands and wash them in his tears.

"You loved enough to—"

I would have followed you to the end of the world, Matt, to lead you to the cross."

"You have followed me through—Oh my God!"

Matt felt the sharp pain in his head, groaned, and lost his consciousness.

When he opened his eyes again the first gray rays of dawn were creeping timidly into the room. He looked at Emily, who was kneeling by the bed, her saintly face lifted toward heaven. He placed his finger tips gently on the ugly scar and prayed.

"Oh, Father, 'the way of the cross leads home.' I follow." She smiled a smile that recompenses for all pain and sorrow that makes the burden of the cross light with the glory of the vision of the crown. "Emily, how long have you been following me?"

"Almost a month, Matt. I saw you often before I came to eat. I saw you every day. Oh, Matt—Matt—don't. You must go to sleep now, please. We will talk again when you are rested."

"I'll never close my eyes again until I know you are asleep first, Emily."

The nurse who had been standing outside the door for some time stepped in.

"Here is your nurse now, Matt. I'll go to sleep right away."

Nothing

By Carol Hostetler, age 27, Hesston, Kansas
Originally published March 10, 1929,
in the Youth's Christian Companion

The last line of the invitation hymn was nearly finished. "Softly and Tenderly Jesus is Calling." The minister stepped to the edge of the platform, held out his hand, and looked Milt Kenton right in the eyes. Milt flinched and looked away. Everyone in the small congregation, who believed in the worth of prayer, had been praying for Milt Kenton, from the time the revival meetings started. The last night had come, the last sermon had been preached, and the last invitation had been given and now the last measure was being sung, "Come—Home." The minister held out both arms as a mother would to take her child.

"Won't you come?"

But Milt kept his seat. Night after night he had kept his seat. Everyone thought surely he would stand tonight. But Milt wasn't going to stand! He had told himself that over and over. Not even if his friend Tom stood. He had told Tom that. Tom did stand the evening before, and now Milt fought with greater determination.

The congregation was standing and as a last resort, the minister walked down the aisle and went straight to the third from the back seat where Milt was standing, his one hand in his pocket and other hand playing with his gold watch chain. The minister laid his one hand on Milt's shoulder, and stood there fully a minute. The congregation was breathless; heads were bowed in prayer; Milt's little mother over on the other side of the church was crying.

Oh, how handsome Milt looked in his double-breasted stripped suit and satin tie, his black hair lying in perfect stiffness from hair tonic. Emma-Nell Benton thought Milt was handsome; Milt knew she did, but most of all he thought so himself. He shifted from his left foot to his right. He wet his lips and counted the buttons on the front of his coat that he had counted a hundred times before.

"Milt," said the minister softly, "What would you do if you knew this was the last night you had to live?"

"Nothing," answered Milt and prided himself on the emphatic tone of voice he displayed.

"Nothing?" asked the minister. "I am not sure of that, as you are, Milt."

The meeting was closed. Milt picked the expensive overcoat from the seat, stepped into the aisle, adjusted his scarf, and pulled on his coat with a most graceful swing, and left the church with a triumphant stride.

He got his roadster from the side street and pulled up to the church door with a dash. He was going to take Emma-Nell home, but at that moment he saw her getting into Tom's car. Milt's anger rose. A little girl in a red coat and hood jumped up on the running board and spoke in a childish accent.

"Say, Milt, I'm goin' home wif you. Mama said so." And she seated herself beside her big brother.

"You go back to mama." He was going to lift her out of the car when she spoke again:

"No Milt; Mamma said I sud go wif you. We're detting company at our house. Aunt Wose an' uncle Elmer are goin' home in Papa's tar. Please Milt, 'et me go wif you."

She had her tiny arms around his neck and stood on the seat beside him.

"I want to wide in your pretty tar," she said. "All right then, honey, sit down." And with that she hugged him.

Milt loved Bonnie Lee more than any other thing on earth except himself. Everyone simply adored her. All of Milt's girl friends made a big fuss over her and he didn't object a bit. She was sweet and cute, clever and unusually beautiful.

The moon had come up and blessed the night with its choicest beams. The nickel on the dashboard of Milt's car glistened beautifully in the light, much to his own satisfaction. Down the avenue he sped, passed Tom in his old coupe, and turned the corner with a swerve. Bonnie Lee clapped her little hands and laughed with great delight.

"O Milt, ain't we dot fun?"

But Milt did not answer. He took his hands from the steering wheel just long enough to give "babe" a hug.

"Milt," Bonnie stood up on the seat, her left arm around Milt's neck. "Milt....?"

"Yes, Bonnie."

"What did dat nice man say to you in church?"

"O—nothing, Bonnie. Don't mess with my hair like that."

"What was Mamma crying for in church, Milt?"

"O—nothing, Bonnie." Milt stepped on the gas a little harder and again Bonnie's delicious, lifting laugh rang out on the still night air.

"Yes, but Milt—it makes me hurt in here to see Mama cry like dat. Tan I sit beside you tomorrow night?"

"We don't have church tomorrow night, Bonnie. You'd better sit down on the seat."

The child did not seem to hear the suggestion, for her arm clasped her big brother's neck all the harder.

"Why not?"

"The meetings are over. Don't ask so many questions, Bonnie."

"Is dat why Mama was cryin?"

They had just passed the house and Milt turned into the drive, stopped, and lifted Bonnie Lee out and stood her on the front steps.

"Stay here till I put the car in the garage, honey. I'll be back."

Milt sprang into his car and just then the coupe passed. Milt turned his head and watched it go down the street. With a sudden rise of anger he stepped on the clutch and shifted the gear. The car leaped forward like a cat for a bird. He felt a queer, terrible, sickening sensation, at the same time heard a babish voice whine, and saw a patch of red disappear in front of him.

He leaped out, and there—there in front of his beautiful car, in the beautiful, terrible, pitiless moonlight—lay Bonnie Lee with her pet kitten clasped to her breast in her tiny loving arms.

That handsome, strong, proud man wilted like a snowflake on the palm of a warm hand. He forgot his fine suit, his slick hair he even forgot the coupe as he knelt and gathered in his arms, the two innocent lifeless bodies. He stumbled blindly, dazedly into the house, and in cruel breathless agony, laid the tiny bundle on the davenport and staggered to the telephone.

He called Mrs. Stanton's number.

"Is Brother Dunbar there yet? No? Just left? How long ago? Yes! Yes! Catch him if you can. This is Milt. Yes! Tell him—oh—tell him to come over at once!"

He fairly shouted the words over the wires. Great drops of cold perspiration fell from his face. He was sick through and through; sick of sin, and of himself. Everything he held dear a few minutes before seemed to turn to ashes now as he looked upon the motionless body of his little Bonnie.

He touched her, he called her, but there was no sign of life. He seemed again to see her tiny lips move and hear her sweet voice saying, "Milt, what dat nice man was saying to you tonight?"

In uncontrollable anguish, he fell to the floor in a heap and moaned pitifully. He was crouched thus when the door opened and in walked his mother, followed by the minister, his father, aunt, and uncle.

"What! . . . What?"

A hush of terrible deathly silence fell upon the little room. The minister's hand was on Milt's arm. He grasped it like a drowning man clutches a reed.

"Nothing! Nothing!" he moaned. He moaned in broken sobs. "You were right, Brother Dunbar. I'll do something, anything, and everything! Oh, Mother!"

He almost crushed her convulsed body in his arms.

"Why—Milt—Milt—whatever happened? Oh, Bonnie—Bonnie, my darling; open your eyes—the doctor—God forgive . . ."

But the little eyes did not open; the face only smiled, smiled. The little black kitten, only slept—slept in her arms.

Mother, father, and son fell to their knees in pitiful, unbelievable, sorrow. The minister prayed.

Milt's voice was tender, remorseful. "Mother, oh, Mother, Bonnie was ready to go and I wasn't. If only I would have stood to-night! God had—to take her—to save me. Mother—Dad—can you forgive me?"

Great sobs shook their bodies—all four. Half for sorrow, half for joy.

"Bonnie, my baby sister, has gone—home—and—I'm coming home, Lord to stay."

Above All

By Carol Hostetler, Age 27, Hesston, Kansas
Originally published April 21, 1929,
in the Youth's Christian Companion

It was Sunday afternoon. The tender blades of grass were lifting up their eager heads for the delicious April shower, while off in the east a rainbow appeared, and hung trembling as if balanced on the tree tops in the woods beyond.

Jesse was standing on the porch watching the miracle with new interest, for that very morning in Sunday school, they had had the lesson of the Flood, and Joe Bartle, the teacher of the boy's class, had taught it in a way Jesse had never heard before. He was twelve, the brightest boy in class, and only a month ago he was baptized and taken into the church. The assurance of his salvation, his close fellowship with God, and the complete meaning of repentance were all new and wonderful experiences to him.

Jesse never had been a real bad boy. He always sat beside his father in church, took an active part in the Sunday school and Junior Meeting, but when Brother Herst started his revival meetings, Jesse discovered that he was lost and the thunder of law shook his heart, and the deep sea of destruction threatened to swallow him up. For the first time in his life, he couldn't sleep. During the last week of the meetings Jesse confessed Christ. A wonderful victorious peace filled his young soul and put a glow on his boyish face that attracted everyone's attention.

"Say, Hulda" said Mrs. Swem, after the morning services, "Ain't it just too interesting, to watch Jesse Mower's face in church? 'Deed and I can hardly keep my mind on the sermon fer watchin'. I never seen such a growed up like change come over a boy his age. It just makes me wonder a lot. He carries his Bible every Sunday and none of the other boys do, an' he even takes notes on the sermons, and Jonnie says he keeps it out an' reads it when Miss Templeton ain't lookin', then don't know his history lesson; an' Jonnie says he hangs 'round the corner of the schoolhouse at recess an' talks to the big girls 'bout such things as the Holy Ghost, an' baptism, and restitution. What does he know 'bout restitution, anyway, a boy his age, an'—"

"Well, I'm sure—""

"An, Jonnie, he's kind 'fraid o' him. He says he sits and gazes out the windows so, an' asks the queerest questions in English class, an' George says the other boys don't have a chance to say much in the Sunday school class, an' Joe Bartel just helps him along. Joe took him 'long home last Sunday for dinner, an' Joe's mother said they sat out on that old log back o' their chicken house all afternoon; an Joe had to spend twice as much time on his Sunday school lesson ever since. An' Jonnie said last Friday in school, Jesse leaned back in his seat an' whispered somethin' to hisself and sorta smiled, and Miss Templeton asked him what was the matter an' he said right out, 'Oh I'm saved.' Now, don't—"

"Well, bless his heart.," spoke Hulda tenderly. "What a wonderful—"

"You thinks that's natural, Hulda?" broke in Mrs. Swem excitedly. Her voice was getting higher and higher. Nearly everyone had left the church. "Why such actions can't last Hulda. He acts wors'en than old Mr. Kerdie did when he came back into the church. I think it's workin' on the boy's mind, so I do."

"Oh, no, Mrs. Swem." Hulda's voice was rich with assurance. "Jesse is, and always was a remarkable boy. I think it's the most beautiful experience I've ever seen in a child. It does my soul good. I think you ought to let John and George associate with him all they can. If only more of us had a hold on God like Jesse has. I want to learn to know him better. Joe says he's a marvel."

Mrs. Swem opened her eyes wider than ever. Her mouth fell open.

"We're goina to take our lunch over to the falls some Sunday," added Hulda, "and take Jesse along."

"Oh, are you?" Mrs. Swem cleared her throat and walked away.

Joe Bartle was waiting outside the church for Hulda. Besides being a devout Christian, he was well-to-do and the report was out that he intended to send Jesse to academy as soon as he finished the eighth grade. Jesse was going to prepare for the ministry; because, as he told Joe Bartle, "I didn't choose my life work, but God chose it for me. I'd rather preach than go hunting, Mr. Joe. I feel it in me."

The rain ceased late in the afternoon. The rainbow in the east disappeared as quietly as it had appeared, and Jesse started down the road that pleasant Sunday evening toward the schoolhouse half a mile away. The farther he walked, the faster he walked, and when he reached the schoolhouse, he leaped up the steps, opened the door with a swing, and closed it quietly behind him. He stood for a long time viewing the empty seats thoughtfully. He walked up and down all the aisles with his hands in his pockets. He stood up in front facing the seats for some time, then walked to the third seat in the second row, stooped down, took out a small Bible and returned to the floor in the front.

He threw back his head, jerked his right leg and smiled strangely.

"I greet you on this beautiful afternoon, friends, in the name of Jesus, our Savior and Friend." His voice was clear, but a little timid. Color rose in his face. He stopped, took a deep breath, laid his Bible on the teacher's desk, and ran his hand through his hair.

"I—this is my first attempt at preaching, friends—but it won't be the last one—and God will tell me what to say. He knows my heart."

The empty room echoed the words in his ears. The empty desks made no response. It was so quiet. Beads of perspiration stood on the boy's forehead, but he did not feel them. He wet his lips and went on.

"I'm going to preach today about Noah, the man who obeyed God's voice and built the great ark. Say, it must have taken a lot of trees to build that big boat, but God made the trees ready, gopher trees they were, and Noah did what God told him to do. Noah walked with God, it says, and God did the directing and Noah did the doing, and Joe Bartle said that's what God's for—to boss the job. Say, I'm going to let Him boss my job; then the waters of sin can't come trickling in the cracks. Noah put pitch inside and outside the ark and that's the . . . obedience makes us safe, you know, and Noah was six hundred years old when the flood came, but he wasn't as old then as old Tom Gundy, because they lived long in those days. You can read all about it in Genesis, Friends; just turn to the sixth and seventh and eighth chapters and read how the birds came flying from all directions two by two, and lions and tigers and elephants and wolves walked and crawled up the plank board into the ark. And they never fought with each other. No, sir, Joe Bartle said the Spirit of God was upon the scene; but it was all because Noah was obedient and let God boss the job. He loved God; loved Him above all. Here's a verse I learned today. 'He loves not God, who loves not God above all.' Joe Bartle composed it himself or got it out of a book."

Jesse turned to the blackboard, picked up a piece of chalk and wrote the verse on the board in awkward handwriting. He turned to his imaginary audience once more and held out his hand and said tenderly, "Friends, do you love God above all? Do you love him at all?"

The door opened and in stepped Miss Templeton, flushed and a little excited. She seemed in a hurry.

"Do you love Him at all?" The words sent a peculiar chill through her body. What in the world? Then her eyes fell on the quotation on the blackboard. She read it with a glance.

Jesse stood speechless. An almost deathly parlor crossed his face. Miss Templeton noticed it and spoke quietly.

"I beg your pardon, Jesse, but I lost my watch. I've hunted high and low and I thought maybe I left it in my desk Friday night."

She walked to the desk and opened the drawer.

"Oh here it is," she almost shrieked with delight. "Did you find it Jesse? Oh I'm so glad."

"No, I didn't, Miss Templeton. I didn't have the drawer open. I just came up here to—"

He could not finish his sentence. He was embarrassed. How could he tell her he came up to the school to preach? He didn't want anyone to know.

Miss Templeton adjusted her watch with trembling hands, and her lips were quivering. She walked over to the window, took the shade cord in her fingers and fumbled with it nervously.

"Jesse" she said without turning around. "Where—where did you get that verse you wrote on the board:"

"I learned it in Sunday School today. We had the lesson of the Flood and did you see the rainbow a while ago over the east? My, it was great!"

"No, I didn't notice it. Jesse—Oh, I wish I were young and happy and carefree like you. Oh, how I wish—""

"'He loves not God at all, loves not God above all.' If that is true. I—I—Jesse, ever since last Friday, I've been troubled—ever since you said, 'I'm saved!' I don't seem to know half the time, what I am doing. I guess that's how I forgot where I laid my watch. I—Oh—" She sank into the nearest seat and laid her head on the desk. Jesse was excited, almost frightened. Never had he seen Miss Templeton loose her composure. Now she seemed only like a little girl in trouble.

"Why, Miss Templeton."—Jesse's voice was almost a whisper. He reached to her desk and picked up the Bible and turned to John three and read the sixteenth verse. "It's so simple, so easy. I thought it would be hard, but it's not, Miss Templeton. Just open your heart and let God come in and then you've got to love Him above all. You'll just have to, and then you'll be happy and care-free too. He wants first place or none at all. That's loving Him above all."

Miss Templeton raised her head. "Jesse—may I go along to church with you tonight, and—and do you think they might give an invitation?"

"Oh, they will. I'll tell—Oh, yes, they will. Do come along home with me now. Mother would be glad."

"No, don't Jesse. Leave it here. Tomorrow morning I'll tell the pupils I love him above all—Jesse, let's go."

Use Your Head

By *Carol Hostetler Kauffman, Age 27, Minot, North Dakota*
Originally published July 21, 1929,
in the Youth's Christian Companion

The clock below struck twelve. Reggie hadn't slept any yet. It was hot, very hot. The one window in the smaller upper bedroom was raised to its highest possibility, but if there was any breeze stirring that night, it missed entrance through the window in Reggie's room.

A frayed and sorely faded quilt hung in rope fashion over the foot of the green iron bed, where the boy had kicked it in a desperate effort to relieve his sweltering body. He rolled on one side of the bed to the other; he pushed the oppressively hot pillows to the floor and stretched out in a new position. He almost fell asleep several times, but never quite. He felt faint from heat. It was waving, bearing, pushing down upon him from the low ceiling; it was suffocating him. It was enough to make one restless, even furious, especially a boy of fourteen, who loved the out-of-doors breeze—plenty of it on his face, wet grass on bare feet, rain, the swimming pool. And tonight—the letters lay on the little dresser. Oh, he could not sleep!

Perhaps something in those letters made the night seem unreasonably heavy to him. Surely it was getting hotter every minute. Perhaps he had a little fever. He tossed again, drew a deep breath, and got up and turned on the light. He unfolded the one letter and read again the two pages:

Blueville Sanatorium
Blueville, Texas

My Dear Reggie,

I am feeling a little better today. They propped me up in a wheel-chair and took me out on the balcony for a while this morning. I could look down over the pretty lawns and see the children playing and hear them laughing, and see women working in their gardens. Made me homesick for you and Daddy, and to get out and work. Made me hungry for strawberries, but I can't have any. I saw a boy ride past on a new bicycle and it made me think of you and how much you want one. But if you work this summer and help Daddy get the hospital bill paid, I am sure we can get you one for Christmas.

I have to stay another month. Then I think I can come home and make you a cherry pie. Daddy said you miss me most at meal time. He said Mr. Linn told him you were the best boy they had in the store. He said he knew he could trust you, but he didn't always trust Tim. It makes me so appreciative of you, Reggie.

Is Daddy working too hard? Of course he wouldn't tell me. Oh, I am so anxious to get well again and come home. Are the wrens there yet? Take good care of yourself, Reggie, and keep the grass clipped along the hedge. Write and tell me everything. Be happy and true like you always have been.

Love, your mother.

p.s. Please stay away from Tim,—Reggie.

Reggie folded the sheets and returned them to the envelope and picked up the other letter. It read:

Camp Jefferson

Say, Reggie, why don't you come? You're missing the time of your life. The water is gr-r-r-eat! So are the fish! What's the matter, scared out? Don't be a coward, Reg. There's fifteen fellows here now and more coming next week. In the water half the time. Sleep right out in the open. Great life, Reg. You can work it like I did if you use your head. It's your own fault if you miss all the fun.

So long, Tim.

Reggie turned out the light but he did not go back to bed. Instead he curled up on the window sill and looked down into the yard below. Now and then a car passed and the voices of joke-seekers rang out through the silent night.

Just two weeks ago, Tim had been up in that very room and showed Reggie how to make a twenty dollar bill out of a ten, by making two's out of thin white paper, carefully working over them with a led pencil and pasting them over the ones. Tim had made a twenty dollar bill to perfection and Reggie had watched him in half-amused, half-dumb amazement.

"And you think you can get by with that?" asked Reggie doubtfully.

"Think so," retorted Tim. "Well, you'll find it out if I don't. Sure, I expect to."

"But look at all those little tens around the edges. You couldn't fool me like that."

"Huh—how do you know but what you get fooled every day in the grocery store? People don't take time to look at the edges. Look," and Tim thrust out his bill triumphantly. "See—not one in a thousand would notice it. And maybe the fellow who gets this one won't notice it and will pass it on, too. Ha! Ha! But it's tough for the one who has it if the two's start peeling off. Let's smoke."

Reggie shook his head.

"Come on, Reg, be a man!"

"Father's downstairs."

"Well, what if he is?" Tim spoke in a sarcastic snarl that made the blood rush to Reggie's face. "S-s-s—you're just a bad boy trying to be good. Come on; let's go to town."

"Can't go to-night, Tim. Promised father I'd go along to—"

"Prayer meeting?"

"Well—I—"

"Well, run along and say your prayers. And by the way, pray for me. I'm going to spend my twenty."

And Tim did. He dashed with an important air into Sidney's cigar store. It was standing full of men and boys. He asked for a package of Chesterfields, laid the counterfeit bill on the glass showcase, and received his change. He then lit a cigarette and stood around and talked a while to choke down his excitement, after which he dashed out with a more important air. "I did it certainly. Why, I knew I could. Ha! Ha! No one in a thousand would notice it. Pretty clever, eh?" he said to himself. And so Tim made his expenses to go to Camp Jefferson and Reg could too, if he used his head.

And this was why, and the two letters were why Reggie could not sleep that hot night in July. He was thinking, thinking, till thoughts were a tangled mass and he was caught inside. His head felt heavy, then strangely light and dizzy.

"Tim—bills—money—money—mother—hospital—fish—Dad—water—cherry pie—coward—thrill—money—freedom—tell Mother everything—store—work—hot—be true—Tim—Camp Jefferson—appreciative of me—He wanted to please—Mother and Father—with the fellows—have a circus—great life—would Tim be caught—could he—?"

Suddenly a light appeared in the woodhouse just below him. From the small window it shone out on the grass. A peculiar feeling sent a thrill though Reggie's tired body. He sat rigid and tense. His breath came in uneven gasps.

"Who could be at the woodhouse at one o'clock? What is in there that anyone would want? There is nothing in there but wood and garden tools. I'll, I'll go down and tell Father."

He quickly descended the stairs. The door of his father's bedroom stood ajar. He slipped in quietly and called.

"Father!" Louder. "Father!"

There was no response. He snapped on the light. The bed was empty! A startled expression crossed the boy's face, while terrible imaginations tortured his already crowded mind. He found himself shivering, while small beads of perspiration stood on his forehead. He really was ashamed of himself for being a coward but—. He slipped to the back door. It was open and through the screen door of the wood-shed he saw the front of a man in overalls bending over a low work table. Without making a sound, Reggie approached the door of the shed.

"Father!"

The man at the table jumped as if struck, and the screw driver he held in his hand fell to the floor.

"I thought you were in bed."

"It's too hot to sleep. Saw the light on and came down to see who it was. What are you up to Father?"

A faint half-disappointed smile played around the man's lips and gray eyes twinkled a little. At the same moment Reggie spied in the corner of the shed, a black, double-barred bicycle, and on the table an opened can of blue enamel.

"Thought I could surprise you—and—now you had to come and catch me before I got finished."

"Why Father—you—you know you couldn't afford—."

"Well, Reggie, it isn't a new one, but I thought I could make it look pretty nearly like new with this." He picked up the can of enamel and a small brush from the table. "I want you to have it as bad as you do. Can't forget how I wanted one when I was a boy—and never got one—and—."

"But Father, Mother can't come for another month—and—."

"Well, Reggie, we can manage it somehow, I think, you and I together. Mr. Lind told me yesterday you were doing fine at the store; a boy he could depend on, and he's going to give you a raise Saturday, and if you give up your vacation and work all summer you—you deserve it, I guess."

A sudden light crossed the boy's face. He walked over and laid his hand on his father's shoulder.

"Thanks, Father. I—I—here, let me paint it. You go back to bed. It's after one."

"Do you want to yourself?"

"Bet your life I do. I'll do it tomorrow right after work. I want to write a—."

He did not finish his sentence, but walked toward the door of the woodshed.

"Come on in Father. You need your rest."

"Dear Mother," wrote Reggie a few minutes later.

You can depend on me doing my best at my job and helping Father, and clipping the grass, and everything. I'm getting a raise Saturday, and Father got me a second-hand bicycle and we're painting it up like new and Tim's gone to Camp Jefferson so I won't see him all summer, and I'll try my best to be true, Mother. Now I guess that's everything. We sure want you to come home soon.
Reggie

Dear Tim,

You needn't look for me because I'm stickin' to the job you left and I'm making half again as much as you did, and you may think you're having a great life, but take my advice and don't be so smart about those twenties, because there are some smart people, smarter than you. My Dad is the smartest and best man on earth and I'm staying here to help him all summer. So don't look for me, Tim. I say, Tim, use your head.
Reg

So This Is Cleveland!

By Carol Hostetler Kauffman, age 27, Minot, North Dakota
Originally published August 18 and 25, 1929,
in the Youth's Christian Companion

The manager of the Adams Defelt Company laid his wet pen on the desk. He then shoved back the paper on which were scribbled a mass of figures, tilted back in the swivel chair, and, thrusting his hands into his pockets, turned sharply about and looked down into the street below.

It was ten minutes till eight in the morning. Men and women were hurrying to their respective places of business. There were old men, young men, middle aged men, old women, young women; elderly maiden ladies in girlish clothes; girls, hundreds of them, in bright colored frocks and shop faces, stealing a view at themselves in the plate-glass windows, running to catch the street cars; girls in frightfully short dresses and furs; laughter, giddy laughter; the sound of French heels on the pavement; the smell of cigarette smoke, girls smoking!?

"So this is Cleveland," the man spoke to himself. "O what is the world coming to? Is there any good? Are there any good women in the world today?"

A step was heard on the stairway leading from the main floor into the office. John Greenaway turned abruptly. An agitated expression crossed his face.

"Another flapper, I suppose," he said to himself.

Already that morning nine girls had called at his office in answer to the advertisement in the paper the evening before. And John

Greenaway had turned down every one of them without even as much as taking their phone number in case he might consider them, and he would turn down this one too, quite likely. He was surprised at himself the way he could talk to these pretty young things, without the least bit of pity. He stiffened his shoulders and—

On the top step stood a girl in a black tailored dress with white color and cuffs. She wore a neat black bonnet, and in her hand she held a black brocaded hand bag and a pair of silk gloves. A delicate half-sad, half-wistful smile played about her lips and she looked straight into the manager's eyes.

"Good morning."

"Good morning Miss."

He did not offer her a chair, and he did not extend his hand, he did not move.

"I'm interested in answering the advertisement in last night's paper, or have you hired someone already?"

"No. No, I am a little hard to satisfy, I guess. A man my age, you know, my nerves are a trifle shot—I am quite particular with whom I have to work with day after day."

"And you have the right to be."

"Well, you are the first girl to give such an answer."

"I can appreciate your position, I am sure. And if I can't fill your vacancy, I shall not be insulted if you say so. I am rather a peculiar girl, I know."

"What's that—peculiar?" The man eyed the girl closely. Her face was clean and a little flushed and he could see from under her bonnet that her hair was long enough to be coiled. And her dress was fairly below her knees.

"Peculiar—yes, that is singular—different from the other nine who called before you. Take a chair Miss—?"

"Greenaway, sir."

"Greenaway,—that's my name."

"O how fortunate! That's not a common name, I find. It will not be so difficult for me to remember."

"How old are you Miss Greenaway?"

"Twenty-one."

"And you've had other office experience?"

"Two years with Mr. Forbs at the Jay Stamp Incorporation."

"You have? And why did you leave, may I ask?"

"I agreed to work for the length of time when I went there, until Mr. Forbs' daughter finished her business course. She is working for her father now. I have here my recommendation from him."

"Never mind about the paper. I'll have you take a little dictation."

She did so with ease and typed it without an error.

"Now, Miss Greenaway, you may call up Mr. Baldwin at the Martin Motor Company, and ask if my car is ready, and how soon they can deliver it."

The manager of the Adams Defelt Company busied himself with some papers on his desk, and he was not thinking about the papers at all. He was listening with undivided attention to the voice on the telephone. It rang out in rich youthful tones like music with a certain distinctive expression, half girlish, half womanly. She pronounced her words distinctly and with singular choosing. Mr. Greenaway sat spellbound, tense. His breath came in quick gasps that almost stifled him. His hands were trembling.

That voice, that voice, something about the girl's mouth and eyes—O he dared not look at her long, yet he could not look away. That voice—he wanted to hear it again—all the time. She turned to the man.

"Your car will be delivered at ten o'clock, Mr. Greenaway."

"O, what's that? Yes, thank you. Would you like to start work at once, Miss Greenaway?"

"I—yes, I can."

"And would you be willing to start in on $20.00 dollars a week with the understanding that if your work is satisfactory, you will get a raise in two weeks?"

"Willingly, Mr. Greenaway." She pulled off her bonnet and gave her head a little toss. Her soft dark hair fell in pretty waves around her flushed face.

"You—may—put your wraps in here. Pardon me; I am a little nervous and worn out this morning."

The girl could not understand the peculiar look the manager gave her. It was not a stern look, but rather a look of astonishment.

"What kind of man is he, anyway?" she mused. "He said he was hard to satisfy, but I'll try—oh, I'll try. Twenty dollars to begin on!"

The manager had left the room. The girl went to the phone.

"Mother, I have a position. Yes, yes mother. No, I'm starting right away. I'll be home for lunch—I don't know yet; I think so. And listen, Mother, $20.00 a week to start on. Yes, you won't have to take in so much sewing then. Yes, good-bye Mother."

"Now Miss Greenaway, the first thing I'd like to do is to fill out this bond paper and give it to the young lady in the office across the hall. Then we are ready to begin."

The morning passed rapidly. The girl threw her whole being into her task and did not notice that several times her new boss stared at her intently, while a strange, sad expression seemed to deepen the already deep line about his face. His bent shoulders seemed to bend a little more and yet, whenever the girl spoke or whenever she laughed, something sent a thrill through the man's body and made him feel young again. O youth, O glorious, alluring youth.

"I—I dare not think—I—" mused the man to himself.

**

Sunday afternoon, Janice looked up from the book she had been reading. "Say, Mother, the man in this story just reminds me of Mr. Greenaway. I think he's the dearest old man. I just love him."

"O Janice, I don't like to hear you say it. Girls now-a-days just take up with anyone. I hope you can always act reserved as I have taught you."

"Why, we are reserved, Mother, both of us—perfectly. Why, Mother, I just love him like I would an uncle. He just reminds me of

Uncle Pete sometimes. He looks so sad sometimes and yesterday I saw him take some pictures from his inside coat pocket and look at them a long time and put them back. I wonder if he is married. He never says a word about a wife. I wish Uncle Pete were living—but Mother, I'm glad to have you."

The girl crossed the room and kissed her mother. "And I'm glad I've got you, Janice. You're all I have in the world, just you, dear. I remember well when you were but a tiny babe. All the experiences that have come to me since then, and all the sacrifices I have made to raise you to God's honor, have made you very dear and precious indeed. You have become my stay now. But for God and you, I could not go on. Eighteen years ago—"

"Don't, Mother—please, Mother, let's go out for a walk. God made the day so beautiful for us."

They stopped on the Johnson Avenue Bridge to look down into the clear sparkling water, when a large sedan passed and a man lifted his hat, revealing hair of steel gray.

"O Mother, that was Mr. Greenaway. He looks so handsome."

"I didn't notice, Janice, I had my back turned."

The next morning the manager dictated a few letters and complained of a severe headache. "Miss Greenaway, I believe I'll go across the street to get something for my head." He walked to the closet to get his coat. The girl noticed he tottered a little.

"O Mr. Greenaway, let me get your coat for you."

She held it for him and settled it around his bent shoulders. "There now; is there anything else I can do for you, your hat?"

"Thank you, Miss Greenaway, thank you. You're doing something for me all the time. I never saw any one so obliging."

"O, it's just the little homely things,
The unobtrusive, friendly things,
The won't-you-let-me-help-you things
That make our pathway light."

The man in the overcoat let his mouth fall open and he grabbed hold of the chair in front of him.

"Why, Mr. Greenaway, are you sick? Are you—"

"No, no, never mind—that poem—a—the rest of it—a—go on."

The girl smiled revealing white, even teeth.

"And it's the jolly, joking things,
The never-mind-the-trouble things,
The laugh-with-me-it's-funny things,
That make the world seem bright."

"Go on! Go on!" The man's face was ashen, and the hat in his hand fell to the floor.

"Are not the little human things,
The every-day-encountered things,
The just-because-I-love-you things,
That make us happy quite?
"So here's to all the little things,
The done-and-then-forgotten things,
Those of-it's-simply-nothing things,
That make life worth the fight."

The man stood spellbound as though he had heard the voice of the dead. At last he spoke in a husky voice: "Miss Greenaway, where did you get that poem?"

"Oh, Mother taught it to me when I was just a little thing. Sometimes we would say it together, and then Mother would always cry because she said my father gave her that poem when she was a girl."

"He did?" A strange light came to the man's eyes. "Your father did? But why does your mother cry?"

"Why. Mr. Greenaway, because he isn't there to hear it. He—he died when I was only three. It was terrible. Mother is the only living relative I have. It was so strange and mysterious, and Mother had not one to write to. We are all alone in the world in a strange city—and—"

"And your father?"

"O I scarcely remember him. I remember once when he took me for a ride on a pony when we lived in England yet."

"England!"

"Yes, why Mr. Greenaway! You are white. Are you sick? You had better sit down while I get a drink for you."

After the girl had left the room the man drew from his inside coat pocket, two small, faded pictures. He looked at them while great beads of perspiration came out on his forehead. He crossed the hall and opened the door.

"Miss Brown, I'd like to see the bond papers Miss Greenaway filled out last Monday, please."

"'Janice Marie Greenaway—Janice Marie—Born Sept 10, 1905, Louton, England. Mother Worothea Bell—seamstress, 129 ½ Belmont Ave. Father dead'—My God. My God!"

He crossed the hall and closed the door behind him. Almost immediately the door was opened.

"Here you are, Mr. Greenaway. Drink it while it is nice and cold."

The man took a sip and put the glass on his desk. She could see he was excited.

"Miss Greenaway, how did your father die, may I ask?"

"He was drowned on our way over from England. Mother said there was a terrible storm. I remember a little. Mother and I were let down in lifeboats and Mother fainted. She doesn't remember everything either, only we never saw him again and—"

"No, you never saw him again. He was unconscious too, let down into another life-boat, carried off to a hospital, later informed that his wife and baby were drowned—read it in the paper—believed it after he gave up all hope—all hope—O hideous thought—lost for eighteen years.

Janice—I—Janice—I must be your—. Look—who is this?" He handed her the two faded pictures.

"What? What? The pony—mother—what? You are my—my father? Not dead?"

The man held out his trembling arms. The deep lines of pain and grief seemed to be transfigured into lines of joy, the joy, the joy that comes of sad, sweet, waiting, of prayers answered, and unanswered.

"Your father, Janice, all that's left of me."

After a moment he walked to the window and looked into the street below.

"So this is Cleveland. Janice, last Monday I stood at this same window and looked down into the same street and spoke those same words, but I was sad and discouraged then. I thought then nothing good could come out of this streaming, tangled mass of humanity; but now the strangest, the sweetest, the most blessed thing that ever happened in a man's life has come out of it. O Janice, my little Janice, God has been good to us. The angels sent you to me. Let's go to Mother."

Rich Without Money

By Carol Hostetler Kauffman, age 27, Minot, North Dakota
Originally published September 21, 1929,
in the Youth's Christian Companion

If you were given the privilege to make a wish come true, would you wish for money? How many of our dreams would require money to be fulfilled? There are dreams that nothing but money could buy. But there are dreams far more beautiful and practical, which can be realized without money, which in fact no amount of money could buy, yet if realized would be the very richest of blessings.

The richest people in the world are rich without money, richer by far, than those with all their wealth. Many a millionaire is actually poverty stricken in the riches of life. The value of a man is according to what he himself is, not according to what he gets in his pay envelope nor how much land he owns. A large estate, or a huge bank account, or wealthy parents, never made a rich man. They only made his pocketbook heavy. Wealth, land, jewels, cars, gowns—the very things people are striving the hardest to gain are the very things that bring them the most trouble and worry. Yet they want more.

Some of the richest persons I know are: the one who has a noble soul inside a calico dress, or inside a threadbare suit; the one who has a radiant smile beneath a last year's bonnet, the one who can look the millionaire right in the eye and smile, and say, "I'm happier than you with all your wealth, even though my body aches from hard work, even though I haven't had a piece of pie for a month, even though I walk two miles to town while you drive past in your $7,000.00 car, because all's well; I haven't the care nor worry that attends to riches, because I have a King who provides all my needs, because I have a peace in my heart all your gold could never buy."

It is the mind that makes the body rich. One of the richest girls in the Middle Western states lived in a little shack and lay flat on her back most of the time in severe pain. Yet, she was known near and far for her cheerfulness and patience in tribulation, growing sweeter the more she suffered. I call her rich because in spite of her body, she had a rich disposition a bright, active mind, and wrote some of the most beautiful essays I ever read.

Some people are born with strong, robust bodies, good arms and legs. If you have these and a good sound mind besides, you are doubly rich. Money can't buy human legs; money can't buy a stout heart nor nerves of steel nor a good stomach. If it were possible, John D. Rockefeller would gladly have paid a million dollars to the physician who could make it possible for him to eat one meal with pleasure. He is rich who has a healthy body.

And who would sell his intellect for a pile of gold as high as Pike's Peak? On one of the beautiful boulevards in a western town stands a mansion, the pillars and balcony of which alone cost $20,000. A few years ago the mistress of that home died in the insane asylum after securing a divorce from her husband. Rich? Yes. Contented No! Socrates said, "He is richest who is content with the least, for contentment, is the wealth of nature."

A certain man several years ago lost $20,000 in a bad investment. He was compelled to sell his lovely home and move with his family into two rooms in a flat. Only those who knew the circumstance guessed there was any misfortune, for no lines of worry nor sadness showed on the man's face and the home radiated a cheerful, contented atmosphere. The mother and father were sweet to each other, and the four little children played on the clean, bare floor, and sang and talked and laughed and ate their jelly bread. Rich without money? Indeed! Rich in love and fellowship, rich in the heart-life and affection, rich in cheerfulness through misfortune. That takes strength of character. That takes soul-stuff. Emerson said, "If the rich were as rich as the poor in comparison, my how rich the rich would be!"

During my high school days there were two girls that made a great impression on me. The one was an only child of wealthy parents. Although she lived four blocks away from school, she often came in her electric car. She wore a different dress every day, and they were the kind of dresses that made you forget what you had been reading, when she came onto the room, so perfectly gorgeous they were. She brought her teachers greenhouse flowers. And tried to make a grand impression, but when she was called on to recite, she never had much to say. She was egotistical, selfish, discontented, and pouted. Today she idles away her time walking the streets clasping her $1,500.00 fur coat with those soft, white, beautiful useless hands.

The other girl came from a family of nine. She walked nineteen blocks to school, rain or shine. She had clothes hardly fit to wear to school, but that girl had a mind so bright and alert, a heart so big, a voice so tender, and a smile so sweet, it turned her shabby clothes into gowns. We just had to love her. She made the best of grades throughout the four years and was graduated with honors. After being a successful school teacher for a number of years, she became the bride of a well known professor, and although they haven't much money, they are rich. To be able to make the best of poverty and keep sweet is a fortune in itself. We admire young men and women who are rich enough in humility to go to school and work their way through and wear an honorable patch on the elbow.

It is another treasure to be rich in carefulness and neatness, so that even though one has few and cheap clothes, they are always neat and clean. The riches of carefulness are not measured by what we have, but by how we keep and care for what we have.

We can all be rich. The world is ours. The trees are ours; the flowers do not stop giving their fragrance when the poor smell them. The sun shines on our gardens as well as on the rich man's. The sun sets every night for you and me. The little bird outside my window could not sing any more sweetly for Henry Ford. The well does not cease flowing, when the beggar stops to drink. It's all ours and none can deny it. We can visit the parks and enjoy passing the beautiful homes on the avenues without it costing us a cent. If we are so fortunate as to live near the lakes and mountains or rivers or the sea, these marvels of God's creation are ours for the looking. What more could we ask?

Those who are only money-rich are rich to-day, and to-morrow they may have nothing, for riches often make for themselves wings, and fly away as an eagle toward heaven and vanish out of sight. But neither misfortune nor robbery nor bank failure can take from us the riches and beauties of nature.

The richest man who ever lived were the ones who made the world better, because they lived in it; men who have lived on and on after death, whose efforts have been an inspiration to help someone live a nobler life.

Wolfgang Mozart, who has done so much for sacred music, was buried in a potter's field. His wife couldn't even afford to hire a carriage to ride to the cemetery, so she and her five little children trudged along the dusty road behind the coffin. A storm came up on the way, and Mrs. Mozart and her babies ran back home. The next day when she went to the cemetery she found they hadn't even marked the grave and she never knew exactly where her husband, one of the world's greatest composers, was buried. Seemingly Mozart left nothing but a sorrowing family in debts, but he left something infinitely richer; the possession and appreciation of the finer and more uplifting type of music.

A rich mind, a noble thought, a beautiful soul, and the ability to express it, does the world far more good than money. Lord Collingwood said, "I can be rich without money by endeavoring to live above everything mean or poor."

J. S. Coffman never had more than enough, yet no one would refute the statement that he has left the Mennonite Church, his family, his neighbors, and even those of us who never knew him personally, a wealth that could never be calculated—that is a wealth of the riches of the Lord, a wealth of peace of soul, a wealth of communion and power with God, a wealth that is greater than an abundance of money, or health, or beauty, or popularity,—a wealth that makes for life eternal!

"Far better than gold or wealth untold are the riches of love in Christ Jesus." "In whom we have redemption though his blood, the forgiveness of sins, according to the riches of his grace." Redeemed, a child of the King, saved without money!

All Things Are Possible

By Carol Hostetler Kauffman, age 27, Hesston, Kansas
Originally published October 20, 1929, in the Youth's Christian
Companion

"Dannie, oh Dannie," Mrs. Albright called to the boy who was raking the front yard. "Come here quick!"

"What's the matter, Ma?"

"Look in the cupboard and see if you can find the camphorated oil—quick. Willie is getting worse every minute. Oh dear, I don't know what to do next!"

The frail woman held the bundle closer to her for a moment, and then lay it gently on the brown and battered sofa in the corner, never for an instant allowing her anxious, weary eyes shift their gaze from the baby. He lay hot and flushed, with eyes half open. Now and then he whined pitifully and twitched with pain.

"Willie—my baby," whispered the mother passionately, "Don't cry, honey. Mother's right here caring for you the best she knows how. What can I—?"

"Dannie, can't you find it? His chest is getting tighter with every breath! I'm afraid its pneumonia. No, no on the second shelf—hurry."

"I've got it ma, but say, it's empty."

"Empty?" she gasped.

Dannie brought in the empty bottle to show his mother. The tiny boy on the sofa cried pitifully and beat his little fists in the air. A hopeless look of mingled agony and despair crossed the mother's face and she smote her bony hands to her heart.

"Dannie, I've just got to have some, if it does cost. Get that fifty cents out of the blue sugar bowl in the china closet. It's every cent we've got in the house and we need it for bread, but take it, bread or no bread, this child needs medicine. Daddy may get home tomorrow, so go to the nearest drug store and hurry, Dannie; I'm frightened. Your cap? Go without—run!"

"Oh Willie," she bent over the wheezing, gasping child in a desperate effort to do something—anything for him. "Dannie will soon be back, honey. I wish I could be sick for you. There—There, Dannie will soon be back and Daddy will be home to-morrow."

Down the street ran the cap-less boy, the fifty cents clenching in his left fist. He was only a block from the drug store when he saw at the corner ahead, a group of perhaps twenty people. They were looking at something in the center, heads slightly uplifted. Someone was shouting. Clenching the silver piece still tighter in his hand and quickening his pace, he neared the edge of the crowd.

"What's up?" he asked under his breath. "Someone hurt?"

Then he saw standing on an empty wooden soap box, a well dressed, heavy-set, young colored man, his black face glistening in the late setting sun, his white teeth shining like polished pearls behind his rippled lips.

"Yes suh, my deah folks," Dannie heard him say. "Ah know su'e as you libin' dat dis is out ob dat to be a standin' heah on de street co'nah, an'tryin t' preach at dis heah time o' day, when you's all in a hurry to get home an' fry dem er tatahs fo' you' ebnin meal. But de Apostle Paul, he says, 'Preach de wo'd be instant in season, out ob season, reprobe, rebuke, exho't wid all long-sufferin' and doctrin'. An' when ah was a sottom' down deah in de rail-way station a while ago, waitin' fo' de six o'clock train, what's goin' to Memphis, (wheah ah's a goin' 't hold a series ob ebangelistic meetin's sta'tin tonight, de Good Lo'd willin') de Holy Spirit, he come ta me an' says, 'Jumbo, while you's a waitin' fo'dat train, you go down on de co'nah o' Fird an' Cla'k Streets bah de side o' de drug sto'e an' say w'at Ah'm a goin'to gib you ta say.'"

Dannie edged his way closer into the ring of inquisitives gathered around the soap box. His two gray eyes were open wide, like-wise his mouth. A heavy-set woman bumped into him, but she was unaware of it.

"But ah says, 'Lo'd—who'll stop t' listen t' me at dis heah time o' day? Why dey'll o'dah me off de street.' An' de Lo'd says, 'Jumbo, you do as ah tells you an' ah'll gib you de crowd, fo' deah's goin' t' be someone deah dat needs a message out ob season. Anyway, ain't it always in season to preach 'bout Me?' An Ah says, 'Yes suh Lo'd ah'm jus youah sur'bent.'"

The young darkie stopped for breath and wiped the perspiration from his forehead and upper lip. No one made any attempt to leave. A few more joined the group. Dannie was inside the ring now.

"Well suh, folks, ah lea'ned may lesson at tryin' t' dodge de boice o' de Holy Spirit to my own sorrow, an' ah said ah'd nebh try it again, so heah ah is an' heah you ah, an' ah da know which one ob ya in dis gwoup o' listenahs it is, de Lo'd has sent heah, but you'd bettah jus all stay lingerin' 'roun', fo' if you go you might be de bery puson dat needs dis heah message.

"Den ah says as I was comin' dwn de street, 'W'at shall ah talk about Lo'd?', an he says, 'Talk 'bout Ma'k 9.23, If dou canst believe, all fings ah possible to him dat beliebef.'

"Now, mah deah people, wh'at is it youah tryin' t' do ob youasellbes anyway? Ah you tryin' t' get ta heaben bah bein' good an' payin' youah hones' debts and keepin' out o' jail? Ah pity youah puhr souls if dat's w'at youah tryin' t' do, fo' deah's on'y one way an' dat's to beliebe on de Lo'd Jesus Christ, an' He can do fo'you w'ats impossible of youahselbes. He can sabe you fwom youah sins if you on'y beliebe. Ah you try'n to buy happiness wif dat ha'd eah'ned filfy lucah? Well's, you can jis spen' all you's got an' all ebah goin' t' habe an' you won't be as happy as de beggah Lazaras, w'at sat outside de rich man's gate fo' de puhr sick beggah beliebed on de Son ob God, an' wah sabed, an' de rich man w'st filled his stomach wif de fat ob de lan' wah finally cast' in de ebahlastin' flames, weah deah was'nt eben a dwop o watah t' cool his puhr tongue. If deah aint nothing too ha'd fo de Lo'd. If you would habe seen dis puhr dahkie free yeahs ago, you would a said it was impossible fo' him to be standin' heah befo'e you all today, fo' ah was as skinny as a fence rail, smokin' five pack o' cigarettes a day., tellin' more lies dan truf, stealin' mah way across de country an' doin' more bad stuff dan's fo' youah good to be a hearin', an' ebwybody who eban knew Jumbo Smith said it wah impossible fo' him to amount to a hill o' beans or be anyfin' but a down-wright wascal. An' it would a-been impossible bah mahself, but a Highah Powah reached down an took ahold o' me an' washed all de black from mah hea't an' put de truf in mah mouf, took away ebery desiah fo' de tas'e o' dem nasty man killahs, put some flesh on mah bones, an' all because ah beleibed on de Lo'd Jesus. Ebah since ah been trabelin' abah dis heah country tellin' folks w'at de Lo'd can da fo' dem if dey on'y beliebe. Ah deah any ob you who de debil has ahold ob, an' youah tryin' to be bettah bah youahselbes? Wall, you nebah can do it. Is deah any ob you who has de blues an' everyfin' is goin' dead wrong an' you da know which way ta tu'n fo' relief? Wall, jis cas' youah bu'den on de Lo'd an' He can make youah hea't as light as a feddah an' change dem teahs to smiles, yes suh!"

Here the colored man stepped down from the soap box and came close to the edge of the crowd.

"Listen friends, ah any ob you goin' home wid an empty purse to an empty cupboard, an' do' know wheah youah nex' meal's comin from? Ah been deah many a time, an' ah nebah gone hungry long yet, logah dan to jis draw me clash to de Lo'd. 'He is fai'ful who promised,' an'ah tell ya all fings are possible if you on'y beliebe. Ah could stan' heah an' tell ma'belous fings de Lo'd has done fo'me, but somewheah down de track mah train's a comin' in.

"But say, do any ob you habe a deah ol'mudah for fadah at home who's layin' on de bed sick an sufferin' an you's tried all de doctah's an' patent medicines in de contry an' dey still lay in beh? De Great Physician say, 'Deah ain't nufin;' too ha'd fo' me if you on'y giv me a chance'. Jis beliebe, jis beliebe, ah say. He came fo' de lame an' de halt an' blin' an' sick. Mudahs, do any ob you habe a little tot at home w'at's sick o' de febah an' no money to buy medicine or sen fo' a doctah? Jes tell de Lo'd all 'bout it a beliebe dat He can heal, fo' de prayah o' faif shall sabe de sick. Ah know cause ah tried it. You habe not because you ask not. Why go along in dis ol' worl' any longah tryin' t' do fings ob youahselbes when de Lo'd can do a bettah job ob it, is you on'y beliebe. Ain't that so, sistah?" He pointed to the heavy-set woman who had lunged her weight into Dannie. "Ain't that so, my lad?" He laid his hand right on Dannie Albright's shoulder and leaned his dusky face close to his.

"I—I guess so," stammered Dannie.

The young evangelist drew his watch from his left vest pocket and replaced it. Turning once more on the group he said,

"Friends ah got lots moah to say by mah train is due in fibe minutes an' ah got to go directly. But let mah final testimony be dis, All things ah possible if you's on'y beliebe. IF you only beliebe." He slipped from the ring and ran down the street.

For a moment the group of listeners stood in dumb wonder, no one saying a word. Then a few started in the direction of the sidewalk and others followed.

All at once the boy, whom the colored man had touched, remembered his errand. The fifty cents was still clenched tightly in his left fist.

"Oh, my! What was to get? What was it? I can't remember. Why, I've been standing here ten minutes, I'll bet, and ma said I should hurry. What will she do to me?"

He remembered the frightened look on his mother's face and at the same time the stick behind the kitchen door.

"Oh, what if Willie is—dead till I get home—and Dad coming tomorrow. What was I go get?" He stood at the door of the drug store for some minutes struggling with his thoughts, but his mind seemed as blank as the stationary in the window. He started home. The words of the darkie repeated themselves over and over in his mind. "All things are possible if you only believe. I do believe it, I do I do." He started to run.

The little mother met him at the door. Her face was even more distressed then before and dark rings showed beneath her eyes. She was ringing her hands.

"Dannie," she wailed, "What has been keeping you for so long? I thought I told you to hurry, and you've been gone three times as long—Oh Dannie! Haven't you got it?"

"Why, Ma, I—I—couldn't re—"

"What, you couldn't remember? Where has your mind gone to? Don't you care anything for your only brother? Indeed!"

A rattling, guttural sound from the bundle on the sofa made the aggravated mother turn abruptly.

"Oh Willie—Willie! Dannie, I'm afraid you won't have your little brother long. Oh, you good-for-nothing, stupid boy! How could you forget camphorated oil—CAMPHORATED OIL!" the shaken mother screamed. "Go back this minute and say it over every step of the way. Camphorated oil! Oh, wait Dannie, he's choking. Go over to Mrs. Jones and call Doctor Ellis to come at once. This child needs a doctor if we have to sell all we have to pay the bill. Go, I tell you!! Don't stand there as though you had lost all your senses!"

"But Ma, I believe."

"Believe what? Oh, for pity's sake—go Dannie!"

Instead of going to the door, Dannie sprang to the sofa and tenderly lifting the bundle in his brown arms, he pressed it to his breast and throwing his disheveled head back, he called out, "Oh Lord, Oh Great Doctor, I believe, I believe. Oh, heal my little brother Willie, and take away the fever tonight, right now, because I forgot the medicine and we have no money for a doctor. You can do it. You can—you can—I know you can. I believe you, I believe, I do, I do!" He sobbed uncontrollably.

"Dannie", his mother's voice was strange. Her face was white. "Whatever has come over you anyway?" She wanted to snatch the child from him. But for some reason she could not.

"Oh Mama, the darkie man made me forget. Be still please—just believe. Oh, Jesus, I never knew You before, but I know You now. I want to love You like the darkie does. He said all things are possible if we only believe, and I do, I do. He said if any little tots are sick to tell You all about it, so that's all Lord. Willie is sick and I forgot the camp—camp—, oh Lord, I forgot but you know—I—I—believe!"

"Dannie," whispered the mother stepping forward. She touched his arm. "Dannie, lay him on the sofa; he's fallen asleep, poor little dear."

"So—so soon? Why ma, I wasn't even done yet. I—I—knew He would, I knew it! The darkie was right."

"What darkie?" asked his mother.

He did not answer her at once. They stood, both of them in mused amazement, watching the sleeping child on the sofa, watching his breath come easy and silently.

"Ma"

"Yes Dannie?"

"What makes your face look so sweet?"

"I don't know Dannie, does it? So does yours! Oh, praise the Lord Dannie, for your childlike faith."

Ten minutes passed and still they stood watching the peaceful child. A faint smile crossed his face as if in a happy dream.

At last Dannie spoke, "Mama, I'm—I'm—kinda hungry."

"So? Ah, yes, I almost forgot, but I believe I am too. Take—yes, take the fifty cents and buy some bread and milk and a little meat."

As he passed out the door, his mother shyly placed a kiss on his cheek. "And, Dannie you're going to tell me about that darkie aren't you?"

"Yes, Mama, while were eating supper."

The Thanksgiving Quilt

By Carol Hostetler Kauffman, age 28, Hesston, Kansas
Originally published November 17 and 24, 1930,
in the Youth's Christian Companion

"Oh Girls look!" Faustine spoke just as she filled her mouth with peanuts from Dorothy's sack.

"Look at what?" asked Lucile, swallowing her mouthful.

"Why, those perfectly beautiful quilts in that window across the street. Let's cross over."

"Let's go," consented the other two. Like three playful kittens the girls scampered, half bounced across the street to do their daily window shopping. It had been taking the girls at least an hour and sometimes more to cover the distance between school and their respective homes. That was in the evening. Of course at noon it required about fifteen minutes, but in the evening it was different. There were so many windows to attract one's attention, especially for these three gay young air-castle builders. There were the new winter coats to look at and criticize. Sometimes they meandered into one of the stores and occupied twenty or thirty minutes time, of a tired saleslady who worked on a commission basis, only to tell her they were just looking. They tried on slippers, too, with no intention of buying any just yet, but might be in on Saturday to decide. Sometimes the furniture stores held their attention, and they expostulated to each other about what they were going to have some day. Then there were the art shops, the floral shops, the pet stores and the jewelry windows, and many others. How could mothers expect eighteen-year-old girls to come home directly after school when they had to go right down Main Street? It was next to impossible.

It had been a little different, however, the last two evenings. For some reason the display windows held less attraction for Faustine, and of course because she hurried along faster, the other girls did too.

"Here, take some peanuts, girls." Dorothy held out her half-empty sack.

"Aren't they beautiful, girls?" exclaimed Faustine, adding "Um-m-m."

"Simply exquisite," chimed in Lucile emphatically.

"They certainly are," added Dorothy.

"They're just the latest thing, too."

"Look at that green and lavender one!"

"And this one in peacock and gold!"

"I'll just bet this is the kind of a quilt Mother told me about the other night," said Faustine excitedly. "She's getting one made for me for Christmas."

"Is she really?"

"I do believe a vine design. Yes, sir! Mother heard about them and went out to see the woman who makes them."

"Who makes them?" asked Dorothy.

"Why, the woman over in Denmore. I don't know her name, but Mother and Mrs. Yoder drove over Tuesday and Mother said the woman does perfectly wonderful work—so neat and particular. She can't make them fast enough. I suppose these are all sold. Oh, yes— the card. They're eighteen dollars apiece. Mother ordered a white and gold one for my room and a green and orchid one for hers, and Mrs. Yoder ordered two."

"Where does she live?" Both girls spoke at once.

"Why, I don't know exactly, in just a little brown house. Everything's clean, though Mother said everything's awful pitiful."

"What's pitiful?"

"The way that poor woman works; and she's had such trouble, too. Mother said I'd be lucky to get mine for Christmas."

"All hand work?"

"Oh, I guess she puts the blocks together on the machine, but the quilting. Just look at it! Such fine stitches and her one hand is all drawn up or crippled or something."

Dorothy was standing closest to the window and looked at the quilts with a sudden peculiar stare. The peanut she was about to swallow didn't go quite down. She turned her fact to the right and coughed nervously.

"I guess Mother got sort o' acquainted with the woman," added Faustine. "You know how she has a way of making up with people. She's been talking about her ever since."

Dorothy was keenly interested in what Faustine was about to say, but she tried desperately to conceal the fact. If it could really be true! They dared never find out. Oh, never! She'd rather die.

"Mother asked if she didn't have any children and the tears fell on the quilt she was working on and she kind o' shook her head and kind o' nodded, and Mother said she went over and put her arm around her shoulder and asked her what was the matter, and she just broke down and said she had a beautiful daughter living here in Orden somewhere, but she hadn't been home for over two years."

"Why?" asked Lucile.

"She doesn't want to, I guess. Her mother isn't good enough for her."

Dorothy fumbled nervously in her pocket for her handkerchief to wipe her nose, which didn't need wiping. She said not a word.

"Yes, and only eight miles away," Faustine remonstrated. "And her mother simply slaves to make those quilts to send her daughter money with which to buy clothes."

"And she never goes home?" questioned Lucile.

"No, and her mother doesn't even know where she is staying."

"Then, how can she send her money?"

This was the first question Dorothy had asked. It was chilly, but she unbuttoned her coat.

"She has a post-office box and her mother has to send it there."

"I'll bet I would!" said Lucile with a decided insinuation of contempt.

"The girl never writes to her mother unless she wants money."

"Well, there must be a reason why she does that way," ventured Dorothy feebly. "Maybe her parents drove her out."

"Oh, I can't believe that answer," answered Faustine. "Mother didn't want to ask much, being a stranger, you know, but the woman was so sad, I guess she told Mother quite a bit after all. But anyway, she inferred that the home was too lowly or the daughter too fine, or she was ashamed of her folks."

"Does she have a father?" asked Lucile.

"Yes, he came in while mother was there. He helps his wife put the blocks together on the machine and has a truck patch besides. Mother brought home some pumpkins and cabbage and she said she's going out there to get things every once in a while just to help them. He's all stooped over and blind in one eye."

Dorothy looked at her wrist watch and took a step backward. She was getting suddenly cold and tired. She wished she were home.

"Mother said they're both homely as mud fences at first sight, but they're both so sociable and sweet she just couldn't help but love them. Why, Mother said she couldn't imagine either of them saying a cross word or doing a mean thing and they're simply broken up over the way their daughter has gone."

"I suppose she'd be ashamed to recognize them if they passed her on the street when she was with some of her fine friends," exasperated Lucile.

"I suppose so," added Faustine.

"Well, if I had a daughter that acted like that." Ventured Lucile, I'd—I'd—"

"You'd what?" Dorothy's voice was forced and a trifle unsteady. She tried to smile and couldn't.

"Well, I won't say. I can't think of anything bad enough."

"And Mother said she takes it so patiently and that she believed the motto on the wall, 'Prayer Changes Things.' I never heard that before. She told Mother they pray every day for their daughter to come home, and she believes her prayer will come true, but she's afraid their daughter will wait till one of them dies. They thought the sun just rose and set on that child."

Dorothy stepped a little closer. The wind blew her hair over her face; a dog walked up and licked her shoe, but she didn't seem to notice. She looked at the quilts again. She wondered.

"Tuesday night after Mother came home and Father was out in the garage fixing a tire, she talked to me a long time. I never talked with Mother before,—really! That is, just to sit down and talk. She's so young and pleasant. And she told me—told me she loves me enough to do that (what that dear old lady is doing for her daughter) for me if she had to. And you know, girls, I've been begging my folks for a new winter coat and I've acted real ugly about it several times too; but after Mother told me about that woman, I said if she got my coat cleaned, I'd wear it another winter, it is the third."

"Did you really tell your mother that, Faustine?" asked Lucile in astonishment.

"You're surprised? Well, I did. Look, she ordered that quilt for me and I know she'll have to pinch somewhere to get it, but she knows I love pretty things. My mother's needed a new winter coat for two years already, and she goes without and gets me what I want. We've had a lot of fun window-shopping and trying on things, but I'm not going in any more unless I want something. I just can't forget about that horrible, heartless, selfish cat of a girl!"

Dorothy's face, which was red, suddenly turned white and rigid. Both girls noticed it.

"What's the matter, Dorothy?" asked Lucile.

"I'm getting cold here. Let's move on. It's getting dark early to-night."

"Maybe I'll get my coat cleaned, too," said Lucile hesitatingly.

"Yours is as good as mine and a little better," answered Faustine.

The trio started down the street in deep thought, but the one who had spoken the least was the most thoughtful. They came to the corner of parting.

"Say girls," spoke Faustine. "Mother's going to take me out there to see those quilts some day during Thanksgiving vacation. Want to go along?"

"Oh yes!" cried Lucile.

"Don't you Dorothy?"

"Oh I'm—I'm—afraid I can't. Thank you just the same."

"What's the matter, girl? You look sick."

"I really don't feel very well tonight. My—my—throat is getting sore. Don't you girls think it's getting awful cold?"

"I don't mind it," laughed Lucile. "So long, Dorothy. Hope you feel all right in the morning."

"So long," muttered Dorothy feebly.

**

"She doesn't act like herself tonight, does she?" The two girls stood for a moment on the corner.

"I noticed she didn't. Well really, we don't know her yet. Maybe she gets moody spells. Where'd you say she lives?"

"I don't know. Down about four blocks, I think. From where did she say she came?"

"I never heard her say."

Dorothy walked half a block past her place before she noticed it. Everything seemed strange to her though she had been going that way for over two weeks now.

She had taken a room in the new home of a young couple, living on the south side of town. I was a much better room, and closer to school than the one on the east side by the woolen mills. Several weeks after school has started, Dorothy decided she was tired of running a noisy machine all day; tired of her grouchy boss; decided she could make more friends in High School and have a lot of fun too. So she registered in the freshman class. What if she was a little late in starting and what if she did give her age as sixteen, and what if she did write and tell her mother she needed twenty five dollars right away? And what if she didn't get the best of grades? She was pretty and attractive. The boys liked her and she had nifty clothes and a clever way of talking. It wasn't anybody's business where she came from or who her folks were. She told several persons she was an orphan, or rather made that implication. Her parents may have been aristocrats for all they knew. No doubt! No doubt!

She had been walking home part way with Faustine and Lucile every evening now for nearly two weeks and they seemed to think a lot of her. She was a good sport, a jolly girl, and always treating. Yet there was something about Dorothy the girls could so far, not understand. She seemed to stand aloof, screened, reserved, in a manner which was rather kiddish, yet familiar.

Dorothy thought a lot of Faustine and Lucile too, until tonight. Tonight! Oh, how could they? Uh, uh! They couldn't know. No—surely—they—uh! Oh, why did Faustine have to notice those quilts in Andrew's window? She didn't know her mother did that. The—the chickens must have been a failure. Two years. Two? A lot of things can happen in two years. She was just sixteen, when she left home—packed a suitcase and left a note on the dresser. She wouldn't go far, just to Orden; but, oh, anything to get out of sight, of that little brown shack and those sickening chicken coops. No carpets, no sink or running water; not even a decent mirror to dress by; no respectable place to have a boy friend come to. She was sick of eating off an oilcloth and having to listen to father read a chapter every morning before breakfast and kneeling down on that hard floor to thank God for things, when she couldn't think of a thing for which to be thankful. And Mother was forever telling her that her dresses were too short, and she put the powder and rouge on too think, and they couldn't afford this and that. Oh, it was terrible, unbearable! She was sick of it, sick of it!

When Dorothy turned back and groped her way up the stairs, she was not only conscious of a sore throat but a sore conscience as well. Half an hour later Mrs. Gordon called for supper but Dorothy announced that she really wasn't hungry and was going straight to bed.

It was the night before Thanksgiving. The pale sickle of the moon hung above the little brown house and tried in vain to outstrip the light shining from the front of the window out upon the frosty lawn. Inside, two bent and toil-worn figures were kneeling hand in hand beside an old, but polished coal stove. A red and white quilt, half rolled was in its frame at the side of the room, and in it a newly threaded needle ready to begin work in the morning. A worn open Bible lay on the table in the corner beside the glass oil lamp.

"Father, I—I—" faltered the woman, "Lets pray quietly tonight," she ended in a near sob.

"As you say, Mammy." He took the drawn hand into his rough ones and stroked it as tenderly as he knew how.

Two eyes, from the face of a beautiful girl, looked in and saw the pair thus. The room was unchanged'—the motto above the table, the same chairs, the same curtains but freshly laundered, the same mother and father, but somehow strangely different. Silver streaked the scanty black and gold. The shoulders seemed more bent, the skin more wrinkled. She saw them get up slowly as if their limbs were stiff and tired. The man took his wife in his arms and kissed her and wiped away the tears with his big red handkerchief.

"It's time to go to bed Mammy." He always called her that. Dorothy had always hated that word. It sounded so antique and uncouth. She had often told her father so. But now, as she heard it faintly through the window, it sounded wonderfully warm and tender. Oh, the whole scene was so sweet and beautiful. They were beautiful too.

The girl's breath came in quick, thick gasps that all but choked her. Every loving thing her parents had ever done for her and said to her came before her now and beside them and all around them, came all the mean things she had said and done, and the meanest thing of all.

A wrap at the door, just a shy, faint, little wrap. The father may have thought it was the wind but he went to see.

"Father! Mammy!" she whispered, "May—oh—may I come in?"

"May? Dorothy, my Dorothy!" cried the woman, and she stretched out her drawn hand and the other one. "May you come in? Oh the Lord knows you're as welcome as—"

"To stay through?"

"To stay? Oh my precious child. The door has never been locked since you left. Let me kiss you. How did you come?"

"I—I walked."

"Never, Dorothy,—eight miles on this cold night?"

"I would have walked, had it been twenty. I'm—I'm—"

"What my child?"

"Oh, I'm sick of pretending I'm somebody when I'm nobody. I'm sick of myself. I came home to ask forgiveness if—if you can."

"Forgive my child?" It was the father who spoke. "As if we might not." Why, he laid his trembling hand on her shoulder gladly—gladly. "And you'll forgive me for being unsympathetic and misunderstanding at times. I know, I—"

"You never spoke one harsh word to me, Father. There is nothing to forgive."

He pointed to the motto on the wall, "It does," he said softly. "It does. Prayer does change things! Oh, what a Thanksgiving we'll have! I'm going to bed now, Mammy. I'll get up early and kill that young turkey."

Dorothy answered with a smile. She could not talk. She couldn't see quite clearly. None of them could. Yet there was in the heart of each a mysterious unspeakable peace. She had never tasted it before. She took her mother's drawn hand into hers, the hand she had always been ashamed of.

"They are ugly, I know, but once they were as beautiful as yours."

"This one too Mammy?"

"Yes dear, until—"

"Until what, Mammy? I thought it was always like this. You never told—"

"I know I never did. I didn't want to make you feel the blame because you—"

"Mammy! Tell me, what did I do?"

"It was wash day, dear. You were two and a half. I had a basin of boiling soup on the edge of the oil stove."

"Mammy!"

"You reached up and took a hold of the edge of the basin and—"

"And what Mammy?" Great tears welled up in the girls eyes.

"I just shoved you out of the way—knocking you down, and the soup went on my hand."

"Mammy, Oh Mammy! How can you love me so!" She could say no more, but the angels knew why she cried. So did her mother.

Two days later, Faustine, her mother and Lucile came out to see the quilts. Dorothy, in a blue checkered apron met them at the door. An unashamed smile made her face more beautiful than ever.

"How do you do girls?" she said as she held out her hand.

"Why, how did you get out here, Dorothy?"

"I walked out night before last. I came home for Thanksgiving."

"Home?" asked the girls in sifted duet.

"Yes, and meet my sweet mother. Mother, these are two of my girl friends. They showed me the way home, but they didn't know it until now."

Lucile and Faustine could only stand and stare. Words could not describe the expression on their faces.

"It was that horrid cat of a girl you were asking about the other evening, but—but I left her in Orden. I'm—I'm different now. I've come home to stay."

"To stay? Not going back to school?"

"Not this year, girls. And if anyone asks about me, tell them I came home for Thanksgiving and decided to stay to help Mother make quilts to help pay off the place. See! We named this red and white one, our Thanksgiving quilt."

Forget Me Not

A Christmas Story

*By Carol Hostetler Kauffman, age 27, Hesston, Kansas
Originally published December 15 and 22, 1929,
in the* Youth's Christian Companion

All said and done! Flossie Brookfield finished the last stitch in the last forget-me-not that hung happily over the very end of the crossbar of the "T" which was embroidered in a rich black. She hung the finished pillow top over the back of the davenport and with arms akimbo, scrutinized the product of her three-days' steady task, and heaved a sigh of relief.

"How's that?" She turned half about and addressed a sandy-haired young man who was lopping over the end of the library table reading the evening paper.

"Pretty nice, Sis," he answered without wavering his eyes from the second column.

"Elwood! You didn't even look!"

"Oh! Yes, yes." He turned abruptly, and thrusting his hands into his pockets, gazed upon the work with boyish apathy.

"Forget-me-not. All spelled out. Is that what you call tatting?"

"Oh Elwood. Of course not. Whoever heard of tatting a pillow top?"

"Well, it's some sort of needle work, isn't it?" I don't know all the terms of needle work, but I'll bet I can name every part of a Ford car."

"No doubt you can, but that pillow top is embroidered! And I made it for Freda."

"Another Christmas present?"

"Yes. And it'll be plenty good enough for her. I don't know as she ever hurt herself making anything for me."

"Did you hurt yourself making that?"

Elwood looked at his sister's fingers as though he expected to see several of them done up in adhesive tape or gauze.

"Of course I didn't literally injure myself, but you know what I mean. I worked at it for hours, and I wonder if she'll appreciate it?" Her voice was crisp and skeptical.

"It would be the first time, Flossie, if she didn't."

"Well. I don't know. Last Christmas I gave her that beautiful cake dish and she gave me an apron. I'm just sure it was made out of a washed-out, chicken-feed sack, an'—"

"That's one you've got on now, wasn't it?" broke in Elwood without apology.

Flossie felt the warm blood rush to her face as her head dropped and she looked down over the apron her sister-in-law had sent her last Christmas, wrapped so neatly, in a dainty holiday box. She hastily folded the pillow top and gathered up her various colored threads. "If Freda made that apron out of a chicken-feed sack , I hope someday I'll find a wife that clever."

"Clever?" Flossie Brookfield looked at her younger brother, with a slightly irritated expression. "That's lack of management. And I hope every time Freda looks at those words on that pillow top, she'll think of all the time I remembered her, since she coaxed Charlie to move out there. They'd be a whole lot better off, if they'd stayed here and Charlie would have kept his job."

"But, he wanted to go too," ventured Elwood. "How soon will supper be ready, Sis?" The boys are coming here to practice that quartette at seven."

This was all said in one breath, as she hurried to the kitchen where she hoped to clap together a few leftovers and make some coffee.

For two summers and a winter, Flossie and her now nineteen year old brother (whom she attentively regarded as a mere youth) had been living alone together in the Brookfield residence. The parents had slipped out as silently as the angels who called them. Mother went first, and shortly after, Father, as if he went to find her and liked it where she was.

The house seemed larger than ever now, and Elwood liked to see the chairs and the hall tree filled up sometimes. It would have delighted him, too, to have had a few of his chums come along home for a Sunday dinner once in a while, but Flossie was never so inclined.

The bitterness of a youthful disappointment had left a caustic effect on her very soul. Because she allowed her thoughts to eat away her happiness, she seemed to really hate to see anyone else happy. Of the few who understood her, her brother was the most successful, but even he at times had to wonder, and chose rather to let her have her way, than to receive a cutting remark or hear an unfair insinuation against his brother's wife. He loved her.

Flossie was an exceptional cook, and almost without fail, had a delicious supper spread on the kitchen table by the time Elwood came in; but at this season of the year when Christmas presents were to be made, the household duties were done in quite extraordinary fashion. Even the plants in the bay window were thirsty a day or so longer. The days were passing all too swiftly. Today was the twenty-second.

It wasn't that Flossie really enjoyed so much making the presents, but it would have been quite too much for her pride not to have given something precisely fastidious to every member of the family. At the same time, she invariably felt a tinge of disappointment (or was it after all gratification) that her gifts were just a little better or a little finer than the ones received.

She was just in the act of lighting the stove, when she heard a rap at the side door. It was such a dainty, quick little tap, Flossie snapped on the porch light, and opened the door sharply.

"Hello."

Flossie did not answer. In the doorway stood a little girl in a blue coat and cap, a bundle of white in her arm.

"May I come in, thank you?"

Still Flossie did not answer, but as she stepped back the uninvited visitor stepped inside.

"Did you see anything of my kitty?" At the same time two big blue eyes scanned the corners of the room expectantly.

"Your kitty?" demanded Flossie Brookfield vehemently.

"Yes. He's black and white, you know. He got losted." The big blue eyes again scanned the possible places of retreat in the room.

"I don't know anything about your kitty or anybody else's kitty, and you may be sure if he found his way in my house, he wouldn't stay long."

"Why?"

"Because, I don't allow cats in my house."

"But mine is just a very wee baby cat, an' don't take up much room, an' he's very p'lite."

"Oh, he is, is he?" Flossie returned in quick reply. "Well. I don't like any kind of cats, big or little and—"

"But you'd like Jack'e. I know, 'cause anybody always does—I ever showed him to. Junior lef' him get out doors an' we saw him run over this a-way to your big house. He likes to run around in big house's. My! Your house isn't as big as ours, it's bigger."

"Yes—yes—I suppose. I mean, where did you come from?"

"Me? Why 'from the land of love, jes' look above.' That's a verse out of Junior's reader I learned."

"I mean, where do you live, child?" Flossie's voice was impatient. "I haven't time to listen to—"

"Why, we live in that white house over there." The child ran to the window and pointed across the street. "we jes' came—not—to-day morning, but the other morning when it snowed a little, you know. An' I wrapped Jackie in this little white shawl, see?" The child unfolded the white bundle she had in her left arm, and held it out before her. "I brought it along so I could wrap him in it 'cause it's getting cold." She shivered a little.

"Well, if you see him will you come over and tell me?" Flossie did not answer at once. The child continued, "Or, jes'come to the door and call Bonnie—Bonnie, real, real loud like that; then I'll run over and get him."

"I'll see—I'll see," answered Flossie feebly.

If you do, then you'll be my darlie. That's what mama calls me when I do something she likes real much,"

"Would you—" Flossie's voice was somewhat softer. She smiled faintly, very faintly. "Would you—like that real much?"

"Oh yes. Then I'd speak you my Twismus piece I'm goina say in church maybe, an' I'd come over to see you every day an' tell you stories- what I jus make up, you know, an' everything, an' everything. Wouldn't we have the mostes fun?"

"I—I suppose—so."

Flossie's face was slightly flushed. "You'd better run home now. It's getting dark

"And—."

"An' you won't forget, will you?"

"No."

"He's black and white, you know, an' he'll like you, 'cause I do."

"You—you do?"

The look of surprise that crossed Flossie's face on hearing this childish confession was not greater than that on the face of her brother as he stepped into the kitchen just in time to hear it too. He had run upstairs to change his clothes and heard nothing of the duet until now. It was such an unaccustomed thing to see a child in the house, let alone, hearing it make such an assertion; it was no wonder Elwood stood stock-still in dumb amazement.

"Well," he finally said, "Who's our little visitor and what's the trouble?"

"I losted my kitty, an'—Oh, that's my mama calling me. I've got to go. Good bye."

"Elwood, go across the street with the child. It's getting dark already."

Without being coaxed, Elwood took the child in his arms, and started down the porch steps.

"What's your name?" he asked gently.

"Bonnie."

"And you say, you lost a kitty?"

"Uh huh."

"What kind was it?"

"Jackie. Black and white." The child picked timidly at the corner of his coat.

"Why, I believe I saw it. It was sitting by the door when I came home and—"

"Oh, where is he now?"

"He's all right, Bonnie. I'm sure. I picked him up and put him in the furnace room where it's nice and warm. I didn't know it was your kitty or that you were after it."

It was just as well he didn't know. Flossie would scarcely have accepted any explanation for allowing a kitten in the house.

"Well, I'll come back with my daddy after it, after supper."

"You'd—you'd better let me bring it over, little girl, to-night or in the morning. Won't that be all right?"

"Uh huh,' she answered reluctantly.

"We're having company tonight, and my sister better not know it's down there. It will be alright till morning, won't it? It's warm down there."

"An, you won't forget?" He voice was wistful and almost whimsical.

"Indeed not!"

**

Could it be that when Elwood opened the door, his sister was humming softly? She stopped abruptly, however, as he entered the door.

"Cute little girl," he thought, as he drew up the stairs.

"Uh huh," answered Flossie, making an effort not to seem interested. She was, through, even to her surprise. If she could have asked herself why, she would have been too modest to answer. Was it something that the child had said? Surely, it was not the cause of the visit.

"When did she come?"

"Didn't you hear?"

"No. I was up dressing. I came down just in time to hear her say she liked you."

Elwood tried to look at the coffee he was stirring and at his sister at the same time.

"Do you want any more bread?"

"Thanks, Flossie, I have plenty."

"Elwood! Look there!" Flossie pointed dramatically in the direction of the cellar door, where stood a small black and white kitten as if debating whether to advance or retreat.

"Well, why didn't you say something about it?"

"You—you—never wanted—"

"Oh, I know I never allowed a cat in the house, but down there out of the cold for less than an hour wouldn't have caused any great objection, I don't believe."

"Well, I didn't know, Flossie."

"And what were you going to do with it, pray tell?"

"I thought I'd take it along to the office in the morning to give it to Sue. She's fond of such things."

"And that poor child! Why, Elwood, I'm glad you came down when you did, so I am."

"So am I, Flossie. I promised to take it over in the morning."

"No, you won't. You just leave it here. She'll be after it. Take it down to the basement again."

"Oh—all right."

The other boys of the quartet came before they were quite eating. Flossie washed the dishes, but before doing so she slipped unnoticed to the basement with a saucer of milk.

She attached the iron and set up her board. The forget-me-not pillow top had to be pressed and packed together with the mittens for Janee, the cap for Bobbie, the kimono for Doris, and a few toys, to-night, so Elwood could mail them in the morning.

"Yes," said Flossie to herself, "This is a beautiful pillow top and I hope every time Freda looks at it, she'll recall all the times I've been thoughtful of her. I suppose it will look like a forget-me-not in a week or so after the youngsters have romped over the davenport the way she lets them."

Forget-me-not. Flossie's head went up and her iron rested a bit too long on the board, leaving a little scorch mark. The quartet was singing. Ross Barney's tenor voice rose rich and clear above the accompanying three.

"Forget Him not, this Child of Hope
That on this day was given
Him shall the tribes of earth exalt,
And all the hosts of heaven."
Still, she listened.
"Forget Him not, this Prince of Peace,
This day let us adore
The Wonderful, the Counselor,
Our great and mighty Lord."

Slowly, Flossie began to press the pillow top. "Forget Him not"— She had a notion to close the kitchen door, but she had a second notion to leave it open. The boys were singing better tonight, than she had ever heard them before. It had never occurred to her before that music could make one feel so—so—well mixed up in one's mind. She could not quite untangle herself. She wondered whether the child across the street would really be back tomorrow for her kitten. She hoped she would. She hoped weakly, too, that the child would not forget her bargain. No one had ever called her a dar—. I mean, no one ever, ever played she was their mama or told her made-up stories or spoken Twismus pieces to her before. Oh, how utterly foolish to allow one's mind to wonder so."

"Forget Him? No!" The quartet drew her mind away from herself again.

"Forget Him? No, but let us spread-
This day His love below;
Our gifts of love to other's give,
And in His favor grow."

They repeated the last verse softly. Softly Flossie repeated the words to herself. "Forget-me-not—Forget Him not—. Our gift of love to others bring." The first bass was having a little difficulty with his part. They repeated the phrase over several times.

"That's hard there," spoke Fred, "That gift of love to others. Let's see, do-ma de-re-la-de-sol, that's it, that's it. That 'gift of love to others."

Flossie folded and wrapped the presents, and on the forget-me-not pillow top, she pinned a crisp two-dollar bill.

When she went to bed that night she felt happier than she had for several years. About midnight she thought she heard something crying in the furnace room just below. She got up and went down. The kitten was curled up on a piece of old carpet by the furnace, fast asleep. She must have been dreaming.

Among the mail that came in the morning was a small square box. She knew instantly it was from Freda. There was also a letter for her and one for Elwood.

Flossie opened the box first. On top was a silk scarf for Elwood with his initials worked neatly on the one end. Under that was something emb—What? Flossie unfolded it with trembling hands. Her face turned the color of the ashes on the hearth, for she lay on the table before her a beautiful forget-me-not pillow top, precisely like the one she had just sent to her sister-in-law a few hours before, only this one was done in slightly different shades of thread and edged in a narrow gold braid.

For some time she stood staring at the work in a haze of bewilderment. She felt almost like crying but she hadn't done that since Father died. She sat down and opened the letter.

Dear Flossie:

The children are all asleep at last, so I'll try to write now and get the box ready for mailing. I won't get it sent off in time, if I don't do it now. I do so want you to get this before Christmas.

Bobbie has been in bed for a week now with a bleeding in his left ear, and Janee is cutting her double teeth. As fortune permitted, I had the pillow top finished before Bobbie took sick, but I worked the initials in Elwood's scarf while Bobbie was napping. He cries most of the time when he is awake, and he wants to be held all the time. I just can't tell you how thankful I am Charlie will be home over Christmas. He came home last night, so I got a little rest. Doris has been a real help to me too. She is quite a little dishwasher already. Of course, she stands on a little stool and splashes considerable, but she gets them done.

I don't know how you'll like the pillow top, Flossie, but I thought of you the minute I saw it. I had several things in mind to get you, but this appealed to me more than any of them. Forget-me-not is so characteristic of you. You've been so thoughtful of us ever since we moved up here. Well, always, for that matter, but I remember especially the kindness you've done the last three years. I couldn't begin to mention them all, but I remember so well how thankful we were for those things of Charlie's mother you sent us.

The big shawl is so nice to throw over the children when they fall asleep. And then that overcoat of Elwood's, you said was too small for him, made Bobbie a lovely coat. And the blue sweater you sent, I unraveled and made two slip-on sweaters, one for each of the girls. No one would ever know, but what they were new. It was so thoughtful of you to send it. It seems like you must know somehow when we need something like that. I could sit here and mention a dozen other things you've done for us, but Bobbie is beginning to whine. I tried to sew thanks into every stitch on the pillow top, remember, you are the best forget-me-not of all. Bobbie is awake now.

My love, a very merry Christmas, Freda

Flossie Brookfield reached in her apron pocket for a handkerchief, but it wasn't there. She wiped her eyes on the corner of her apron instead. She folded the letter slowly and tenderly as though it were something sacred. The fountain of her heart that had been trying to find a way of escape since that night before, suddenly gushed forth.

"Forget-me-not?" she cried, "No—no, forget you not, forget Him not." She went into the bedroom. An hour later the house was empty, but on the kitchen table lay a note.

Elwood—I took the eleven-forty train for Manton. Bobbie is sick and Freda needs me. I expect to stay a week or longer if she needs me. Get what you want from the cellar, or eat uptown if you like. If you can get off, come down yourself tomorrow and stay over Christmas. At least come over Christmas. Charlie is at home. Bring something for the children. Oh yes, the little girl came for her kitten. It made me as happy and it did her.

Flossie

Two Slips of Paper

*By Carol Hostetler Kauffman, age 28, Hesston, Kansas
Originally published January 5, 12, 1930,
in the* Youth's Christian Companion

The sun was just coming up from behind the grove of cottonwood trees at the farther end of the blue-grass meadow. Ralph Winrod watched it apprehensively as he gulped down his last pancake. It was nearing seven o'clock. A faint whistle was heard from the direction of the cottonwood trees, and was followed by an organized yell. No one else in the house noticed it, for only expectant ears would have caught the echo. Without excusing himself, Ralph left the table and got out his four-buckle overshoes from behind the kitchen stove and cast an eye at his "410" hanging on two nails above the cellar door. He was just in the act of standing on a chair reaching for it, when his mother called to him from the dining room.

"Ralph, why didn't you finish your breakfast?

"I did."

"Why, you didn't even touch your cocoa and you said you wanted some."

"Did I? Well—I forgot it."

"And you ate only one egg. What are you looking for?"

"I'm not looking for anything."

"I thought I heard you get up on a chair."

"Well, maybe you did."

The question in the mother's mind was immediately solved, for she heard him slipping a rod through the barrel of his shotgun. Another whistle came from the direction of the cottonwood grove, this time a little louder. They had evidently crossed the creek. Both Ralph and his mother heard it this time.

"You're going hunting, Ralph?" His mother's voice was subdued and full of surprise. She stepped to the kitchen door.

"Yeh." He pulled on his leather coat, trying at the same time to avoid his mother's eyes.

"Where?"

"Down on Fletchmen's timber. I'll bring home some rabbits for supper. There's a lot of them down there."

"How do you know, Ralph?"

"Well, there always are this time of year,"

His mother said nothing, but he knew by the way she stood there and looked at him that she did not approve of his going. He was quite sure he knew why, too.

"Didn't I hear you tell father yesterday you were hungry for rabbit?" He asked not impolitely.

"I did say that, Ralph, and I wouldn't care if you went hunting if—"

"If what?" He had his cap on now, and walked toward the door. A look of sad disappointment crossed his mother's face that hurt him inwardly. Two weeks ago he had felt the same way when he had gone against her wish by going skating with a certain gang of boys. No doubt it was the same gang who had given the yell from beyond the grove, half a mile away. He had vowed to himself on the way home that he would never make his mother look like that again. One of the children just waking from sleep called from upstairs, but the mother did not hear him.

"Eldon's calling, Ma."

"Yes, I suppose so. But he should sleep longer. With whom are you going?"

"Arnold and Dave are going."

"Who else?"

"Well, Bill Bray."

"Who else?"

"I don't know who all is going, Ma. Bill just asked me to go along."

"Is Bill's cousin going along?"

"Well, I suppose so. I don't know."

Ralph opened the door. The boys were just coming across the meadow.

"Did you ask your father if you could go, Ralph?"

"No. I didn't, Ma. Can't a fellow my age, go a couple of miles from home without asking his dad?"

"Not with such a group, Ralph."

"Well Ma, if you can't trust me in a gang with Arnold Welman, I wonder where you—"

"But I see Arnold isn't in the gang. I wondered if his father would allow him to go out with Bill Bray and that cousin of his."

The boys were close to the barn now. Two hounds were walking beside Bill Bray.

"Ralph, I'd much rather you'd go hunting with your father."

"I'd never get to go if I waited for him."

"If Bill's cousin is as careless with that gun he has in his hand, as he is with his conduct, I'm afraid someone will get hurt. You remember what happened to Jake Tompkins's boy last year."

"That was his own fault."

"Even if it was, his mother never got over it. I hate to see you go, Ralph." Her voice was tender and hesitant.

"Ye ho—ye ho," shouted the boys in the yard. "Let's go—let's go."

"It's too late to get out of it now, Ma." And Ralph Winrod closed the door behind him.

"Oh, Ralph!" His mother bit her lip to keep back the tears she feared might come in spite of herself. The phone rang.

"Yes. Yes, he just stepped outside. I'll call him." She went to the door and called.

"Ralph! Someone wants to talk to you on the phone."

"Just a minute, fellows." My, how he hated to go back into the house and probably argue the questions further with his mother. He half wished after all he had told the boys he could not go. Bill and his cousin had used some language he hoped his mother had not heard.

**

"This is Jonas Merkling," came from the other end of the line. "Can you come over and work for me today?"

"Oh. I don't know. What doing?"

"Grinding feed. I got Arnold Welman to come and he said maybe I could get you to help him. What Say?"

"Oh, I don't know. I was going hunting."

"Yeh. Well, that's what Arnold said. He was too, but he said he'd rather have the money, than go hunting. There'll be rabbits next Saturday yet. You're good around an engine. I need you pretty bad, Ralph. I'll give you two dollars. Will you come?"

"Oh—I guess so."

"Can you be here by eight?"

"Oh I guess so. Yes, I'll be here by eight."

"Well, Ma," Ralph turned to his mother, "I guess I won't go hunting today after all. Merkling wants me to grind feed for him."

"Oh, I'm glad, Ralph. I hope you do get to go hunting today, but not with those fellows."

By eleven-thirty, Ralph and Arnold had a third of the feed ground, when a quarter-inch bolt got down in the grinder and broke one of the castings that held the burrs in place.

It was six miles to town. The casting would have to be welded, and since the machine shop closed at noon on Saturdays, there was nothing else for Jonas Merkling to do but pay the boys half a day's wages, and dismiss them after dinner.

"I'd like to have you both come back next Saturday." They both agreed.

"Say, Ralph, maybe you and I can go hunting yet."

"That's what I was thinking. Call me up as soon as you get home."

Ralph found his father sorting potatoes in the cellar.

"Home already?"

"Yeh, the grinder broke. Say, Father, how about going hunting with Arnold and me?"

"When?"

"Pretty soon. I can't go next Saturday, Merkling wants me back again. Come on, father. That doesn't have to be done today."

"Did you know Mother has a birthday Monday?"

"Didn't think of it Father."

"Fried rabbit would taste pretty good, wouldn't it? I'm glad you didn't go with Bill's gang." Arnold called just then.

"Yes," said Ralph. "Father's going along. Meet us at the bridge in twenty minutes."

The three were nearing the edge of the timber from the south side, when they saw several rods ahead of them, four figures standing around a pile of something on the snow covered ground. Bill Bray and his cousin and Dave Brown were in the group, and the fourth person, a middle-aged man, had a paper in his hand on which he was writing something.

"You will appear Monday at nine o'clock," they heard him say. "All of you. You may take your rabbits home, but I'll take care of these seven prairie chickens."

"But I didn't shoot any of the prairie chickens, I tell you!" said Bill's cousin angrily.

"You were carrying three of them and the others say you did. I will hear no more from you. You will appear as I told you, or suffer the consequences."

The Game Warden gathered up the chickens and—

"Why, Hello, Winrod," he called out on seeing the three approaching.

Instantly the boys looked around, beaten and embarrassed. They walked off.

"You can have all the rabbits you shoot," he laughed, "but don't try to get away with prairie chickens this time of year."

"I'd know better than to try that, Sam. I'm thankful my boy didn't start out with this gang this morning. It's only providential that he didn't."

"Would have made it rather embarrassing for you with your position in Church."

"I was thinking so much of that just then, although that does mean a lot; but I was thinking of how it would have hurt his mother."

"I wouldn't have killed any, Father."

"It would have been a big temptation, Ralph. No, I don't believe you would have, but it is better to stay out of such company."

"I'm sure glad my mother said I couldn't go," said Arnold. "I fussed to her, but I don't care now that she wouldn't let me."

A little after dark, Ralph and his father walked in with the six good-sized rabbits and Arnold went home with four. Shortly after supper the Winrod family went to town. Bedsides doing the regular week-end shopping, a few members of the family went home with packages that Mother did not see until Monday evening.

Father gave her a sewing basket she had been wanting for ever so long. Anna gave her a new thimble and little Ben a brand new tape measure, (which to his childish imagination cost lots of money), and Ralph a box of candy he had purchased with the dollar he had earned grinding feed.

Mother opened a box of candy last. As she removed the lid two white slips of paper fluttered to the floor. Ralph picked them up. An astonished expression crossed his face as he stared at them. On the one slip which was about an inch and a half square was perforated the words, "Packed by No. 9." On the other slip which was somewhat larger was written carefully in ink, "Enter not into the path of the wicked and go not in the way of evil men."

"This didn't fall out of the box of candy surely," he said curiously.
"I think it did, Ralph. They fell out together. What are they?

**

He handed the two pieces of paper to his mother and the same astonished expression crossed her face and likewise father's. "Oh, that never came out of the box of candy," said father positively. It just must have fallen from the table."

"It's none of our writing," answered Ralph. He put the two slips of paper in his right vest pocket, sampled the candy and went up to his room.

For some time he studied those two slips of paper, determining in his mind to solve the mystery, if that's what it was. Did it fall out of the box of candy? If so, who put it there? Who wrote it and why? Where is such a verse found?

After much searching with the aid of the concordance in the back of his Bible, he found the exact words in the fourth chapter of Proverbs. He read them over and over. He read the entire chapter. If it did fall out of the box of candy, why should he have been the person to buy that particular box? Who was No. 9? He wondered until he wondered himself to sleep, and he dreamed he was with Bill Bray's gang and was arrested. He was more than thankful to awake and find out it was only a dream. The verse on the slip of paper came afresh to his mind. He wondered some more.

The week passed rapidly, and still Ralph had not been able to discover where the paper came from. He knew the verse by heart now and repeated it daily until it almost became a part of his young soul. The bit of paper was like something sacred to him and the reading of the chapter in which it was found was changing his entire thought life. His parents noticed it, silently rejoicing.

Sunday evening Brother Faber had charge of a thirty-minute testimony meeting. A number of people responded by giving their favorite Scripture verses. A young girl in a blue dress, sitting at the extreme left side of the room, rose slowly and said in a clear ringing voice,

"There is a verse found in the fourth chapter of Proverbs which has been of special help to me in the last months or so, and it reads like this: Enter not into the path of the wicked and go not in the way of evil men."

Ralph Winrod sat straight in his seat, and his hand went to his right vest pocket. The girl was Miriam White.

"Since I have left the farm and gone to the city to work, I find I have many temptations I never had before. It is so easy to forget the instruction of my parents and act and talk like those about me who aren't Christians. Yet I know my parents and the church expect more of me and my desire is to be true, if I have to stand alone and learn to say no.

"And so to strengthen myself, I learn a Scripture verse every day, while I am at work, and I have found it to be a wonderful help to me. This verse, and in fact, the whole fourth chapter of Proverbs , has been a real inspiration to me, and has helped me to say no."

After the girl sat down, Ralph's mind was working harder than he had ever worked with his hands. Then a deep peace flooded his soul like nothing he had ever felt before. He was too happy to sing, so he prayed.

"Miriam," Ralph spoke to the girl outside the church after the services, "I enjoyed your testimony tonight,"

"You did?" her voice was sweet with gratitude.

"It was my testimony, too, although I—I never gave one before and—"

He drew from the right vest pocket the two slips of paper.

"Did you ever see these before?"

She did not answer, but looked at him in wonderful surprise.

"Where are you working, Miriam?"

"At the Ramson-Jewel Candy Factory."

"How long? I didn't know that."

"Over a month now. I—"

"And are you No—"

"I am No. 9, yes, and, and that is my writing to be sure, but how—"

"You put it in a box of candy you packed?"

"Never! I had that slip stuck in the cuff of my dress, so I could look at it if I forgot it. I was trying to learn that one that day, but I don't see how it—You say it was in a box? Did you buy a box somewhere?"

"Yes, last Saturday night for my mother's birthday, and these two papers fell out."

"Well, I knew I lost it somewhere, but I never dreamed it fell into a box of candy. It could have easily, however, and I never would have noticed it."

"You didn't lose it, Miriam. You just passed it on. And you'll never know what this verse has meant to me. I'm still on the farm, but I have temptations, too, and I've got to learn to say no. I'm going to keep these two little slips of paper forever, if I may."

"You paid for them Ralph. I guess they're yours."

Disappointed?

By Carol Hostetler Kauffman, age 28, Hesston, Kansas
Originally published February 9 and 16, 1930,
in the Youth's Christian Companion

The bowl of soup which was making its rounds at the Eaton supper table rested untouched for a moment beside the plate where Father sat. He looked across the table as if struck with a sudden foreboding; then almost as suddenly, the look vanished, for the one who was addressing him was his eldest son, a son in whom he would not hesitate to place his complete confidence. He helped himself to one ladle of soup, and looked across the table again.

"Of course, you are not considering it, Mack!" This was not spoken in the form of a question, but after several moments, Mack answered it, while he kept his eyes on the plate.

"I—ah—yes, I am considering it, Father."

Mack Eaton looked down over the front of his suit in an endeavor to spy any possible specks of lint. He had, whenever he was the least bit excited or strained. There were no specks to remove, but he brushed over it anyway. He took several spoonfuls of soup, but indeed was not aware that it was his favorite kind. And Mother had fixed it especially for him.

She was looking at him now, as he sat there, robust and broad-shouldered, the very picture of vigorous manhood with keen intelligence. Father and Mother both looked at him, and wondered not that he was given first place. Every line and curve of his ruddy face spelled leadership and strong character, though not quite nine-teen, his voice was deep and steady.

"Are you asking for my permission?" Mr. Eaton's voice was not stern.

"Well, not exactly permission, Father. I know you have authority to refuse if you care to. I am asking for your consent. Would you please pass the crackers?"

"I think you know already, Mack, what I think of these class plays, let alone helping to take part in one." Mack made no answer.

"Don't you?" Father's voice was not unkind.

"Well, yes Father," he answered slowly, "I know what you used to think, but we have a different English professor this year, and it's a high-class play."

"That might be, but it's not high-class enough for you, Mack."

"Why, Father, *The Man Next Door* is the greatest little drama that has been written in the last ten years. You ought to read it. It's as good as a sermon. They tried out for characters this morning, and they had three of us fellows try out for the Parson. That's the leading character. They tried out Wilbur Deckton, and John Slater, and me, and the judge's decision was unanimous for me. They told me I was just exactly the fellow for that part. I wasn't going to try out. It never entered m mind, but Mr. Shoeman talked to me for over an hour, and showed me all the advantages, and reasons why I should, and Father, why, it would be a wonderful experience in public speaking, and character interpretation, and memorizing, and besides having the honor of taking the leading character. It is a chance of a lifetime!"

"It's a great chance to resist temptation, Mack." His father's voice was not harsh.

"Don't say temptation, Father. Mr. Shoeman said it's a privilege; and a rare privilege that the class has a member of my ability. He said he wished every class could produce a fellow of my type. Shoeman's a wonderful professor, Father; I've learned a lot from him."

"I believe that Mack. I know nothing of the man, except what I hear from you; but I realize this, that he can probably un-teach in half a year, what I have been trying, by the grace of God, to teach these eighteen—what can it be?—yes, nearly eighteen years.

Mother", Mr. Eaton turned to the woman at his side, "Where is our little Mackie?"

She answered with a tender smile that was lightly plaintive. She looked wistfully at the second son, who was following close in the footsteps of his older brother.

"I hope you do not think that, Father. I am beginning to appreciate more every day, what my parents have done for me, and I do not mean ever to depart from it; but a person should be open to new ideas, and a broader view of life."

"Mack, you astonish me tonight! I had no idea—"

"It's nothing serious Father. Don't look at me like that. I've been thinking a lot for myself of late. And I've been reading quite a bit too, and no man ever got anywhere who never thought of himself."

"But Mack," broke in his father, "are you sure Mr. Shoeman is not doing the thinking for you?"

"No Father."

"At least he's injecting his ideas. Do you remember what I told you when you started to high school?"

"Yes."

"It's one of the greatest problems confronting our church today. I must commend you, Mack, for avoiding the class meetings, and dances and festivals, and I've never heard you once ask to join the athletic association. I say, Mack, I've been grateful more than once, for the stand you've taken, but I'm rather taken back tonight, that you ask to take part in a class play. When will it be given?"

"Well, not until June. But they're forming the cast now, and they want to start practicing the first of March. I've thought a lot about it today, Father, I really have, and this is something different, altogether. It's an intellectual work in the first place, and it's an honor to be in it. No one with an average or below ninety can even try out. And the play itself is a noble piece of work. The Parson is a prince of a man, and to learn to act his part would only inspire me to be that kind of man myself."

"He's not a real character?"

"Of course not, but it's true to life."

"I could give you stories of real characters that you could imitate in everyday life, without getting on the stage to do it."

"Is that your objection?"

"That's one objection. Mack. But it's the principle of the thing for which I contend."

"And that?"

"That we as a church take the stand that it is not conducive to the spiritual life to take part in anything, merely for public or popular entertainment." His father's voice was not stern.

"I agree with your principle. But our interpretations differ. That is my principle, and I mean to be true to it; but this play is not primarily for entertainment, but it is instructive. It has a moral. I would take the part for the sake of helping someone."

"And there is nothing in the play that would detract from that idea?"

"No."

"No jesting?"

"Well, of course, every play has at least one clown. That's life. We even have such in the church. Look at Tom Decker. He never gives a talk without telling a couple of funny stories, but he brings out the point."

"And which do you remember till Monday? The scripture or the joke?"

Mack Eaton smiled weakly and took a drink.

"Mr. Shoeman will be terribly disappointed if I don't take it."

"Not as much as I would be if you do.

"Mack, you've never disappointed me yet."

**

Mack helped his mother clear off the table, and looked at the evening paper. He looked at it. He did not read much, and what little he did, made very slight impressions, for his mind was wholly engrossed with the discussion just ended. Every picture in the paper seemed to be transformed into a stage in the center of which stood the Parson, while crowds of spell bound spectators gazed on the scene with admiration. But beside it all, appeared three faces, and six grieved eyes. They were those of Father, Mother, and Jonathan Wheeler. That alone completely spoiled the thrill of the whole scene. He looked through several magazines, fixed the fire, and worked at his chemistry problems. He wound the clock which had been wound in the morning, cleaned his fingernails and worked at another problem. Quite a while after the others had gone to bed; Mack turned out the lights, and stood for a long time over the register at the foot of the stairs.

"Well, Mack," spoke Mr. Shoeman with a friendly smile as he met him in the hall next morning. "What have you decided?"

Mack ran his long fingers through his hair, and answered slowly.

"I'm afraid I will have to disappoint you this time. I can't do it."

"Can't do it?" The middle-aged man turned his head with a jerk. "You mean to say you aren't able, or does someone stand in the way?"

"Well"—and Mack rested his hand on the knob of the door by which they were standing. "I really am not able to do it because—"his voice was deep and sincere, "it would disappoint my parents—and I would have to go against my own convictions to do it. They didn't say I couldn't, but they said something more forceful than that, and really, Mr. Shoeman, much as I hate to dis—."

"Mack," Mr. Shoeman placed a hand firmly on Mack's left arm. "I—ah—step inside for a moment." He swung open the door.

"Sit down there." He pointed to the swivel chair behind his desk.

For over a minute, the English professor stood facing the boy, his hands in his pocket, his head thrown back.

"Mack, you really haven't disappointed me."

"What?" Mack's voice was animated, and he got up from the chair.

"Sit down," ordered Mr. Shoeman. He came a step closer to his pupil. "I'm going to be frank with you." He drew one hand from his pocket and pointed at him. "Ever since you came to my class, I've been studying you, and reading you like a book. You've got something I—I almost had at one time—that was years ago, when I was a boy your age, and Father was still living. I know quite a bit about the people of your faith. My parents were members of your church. Ah—you are surprised! Some others would be, too, if they knew it, but it's true nevertheless. I was brought up in quite the same fashion as you, I presume. My father used to talk to us boys, until the perspiration came out on his brow. I know for what your church stands, and the doctrines she teaches, but the present age is pulling away from it. Mack, I hate to see it! Even though I am failing myself, I admire true consistency in others. Mack—" the professor's voice was subdued and trifle unsteady, "ever since you came to my class, you've reminded me of John, my youngest brother—size, and build, manner of talking. That's one reason why I have taken such a special interest in you. He seemed to be a father's favorite, and I believe it was because he was closest to him in Christian fellowship. The rest of us boys were inclined to be heady, and self-willed. Well, well John died before he reached twenty. Not long afterward father went—seemed he couldn't stay."

Professor Shoeman walked to the window, and looked out on the snow-covered lawn. Someone knocked at the door, but he made no answer.

"I went off to school and my father didn't approve. I got with the progressive type of students, the free-thinkers, you know. It went to my head. Father noticed it the first time I went home. The second time I went home, I was a little more bold. The third time I went home to—see Father laid away. No, I never did anything downright wicked. I claim to be as ethically and morally upright as any member of our faculty; but I tell you Mack,"—he came over and dropped his fist on the desk—"I'll tell you Mack, I'd give this hand to be where you are today, and live my life over, and be the man my father was.

I have talked to you the way I have because I've been used to talking that way and because—I wanted to really see of what you were made. You never knew it, Mack, but you've set me thinking the last few months, by your conduct here in this school. You are bright, and you deserve that position in the play, but Mack—it's not big enough for you. I asked you, to try you. I made up my mind if your faith and Christianity wasn't great enough to help you say 'no' it wasn't worth considering. Disappointed Me? Mack Eaton, you don't know how thoroughly disappointed I'd have been, had you accepted it. None of us expected you to Mack,"—and tears that lay dormant for fifteen years crept unbidden to the professors eyes, "don't disappoint your parents as I did. I've been teaching English and Dramatics for nearly ten years and I've received praise and honor from young and old, and a fat envelope, but I consider my life a—failure."

The boy at the desk was trembling. He could not control it.

"I did not know, Professor Shoeman, I did not know—"

"Know what?"

"You were like that. I had an awful fight last night—I mean, with myself. I really wanted to do it bad, but I didn't have the nerve to hurt Father and Mother—and—"

The door opened and students started streaming in.

"English class will not recite this morning", announced the professor. "Take the same assignment for Monday."

Some of them looked at each other wonderingly, and whispered. This was unusual. Professor Shoeman did look ill and troubled. He closed the door gently. Mack Eaton was still sitting at his desk.

"Mack," the Professor's voice was strangely tender and pathetic. "I simply couldn't lecture this morning from the outline I made. Not now. You would be disappointed in me."

Adopted

By Carol Hostetler Kauffman, age 28, Hesston, Kansas
Originally published March 2 and 9, 1930,
in the Youth's Christian Companion

It was cold. The wind howled and swirled through the trees at the side of the house, whipping their bare twigs against the window pane every now and then, like some angry unseen spirit.

Agnes looked up nervously and scowled slightly. It was getting cold in the house too. She pinned back a stubborn strand of black hair, and moved her chair a little close to the table. In a few minutes she had the seventeenth invitation tinted, then placed it beside the other sixteen. After adjusting her chair very carefully, she looked once more over the list of names before her, and began addressing the envelopes. The front door opened, but Agnes did not look up nor speak to the boy who blundered across the room.

"Oh, Rich—" Agnes screamed at the top of her voice, and the pen she held in her hand fell on the half-addressed envelope, leaving a blotch of ink on the lower corner, and on the table cloth as well. She turned on her brother indignantly.

"Richard Stem." She snapped, and the strand of hair fell over her face. "How dare you? You mean old thing! Look there, what you made me do!" She stamped her foot on the floor. "Laugh will you? I don't see anything funny at that. Keep your cold hands in your pockets where they belong. It's cold enough in here." Richard only grinned. "You think it's smart to be tormenting someone all the time. I just wish Annabelle would come walking in some time and see how nasty you act around home, so I do! Did you get your manners at the Ten-cent Store, six for a nickel?"

"And did you get that temper of yours at the Blacksmith Shop—just off the iron?" retorted the boy sarcastically. "I wish Tom Smith would come in sometime and hear you spouting off at me. He wouldn't think you were such a sugar-lump."

"Oh be still. He'd think you were cruel for ramming your icy hands down my back, so there!"

"Agnes," Mrs. Stem stepped in from the direction of the kitchen and spoke in a low voice, while she tied on her apron. "Are you quarrelling again?"

"It takes two to quarrel, if I know anything! Look there, Mama, at what he made me do on your good table cloth and that envelope is simply ruined. He deserves a good bawling out, and if you don't give it to him, I'll see that he gets it. I might catch my death of cold. He thinks he can just—"

"There, there Agnes. You're just working yourself into frenzy. I wish you could—"

"Well," stormed Agnes, "when Richard learns to behave himself, it won't be hard to control my temper."

"Richard," spoke the woman stepping close to the boy, "you'll soon be a man and I hope you'll soon learn to act like one. Go down and look at the fire, and bring up a few sweet potatoes."

Mrs. Stem put her hand on the girl's shoulder and looked at the invitations spread out on the table.

"They look very nice, Agnes, I think you can erase that ink spot. Are these the names you've decided on?" She picked up the card and looked at it in a moment. "And you're not going to invite Annabelle Tison?" she asked.

"No, I'm not."

"Here's your spuds, mama. Where do you want them?"

"In the sink, Richard."

"But she's in your class, Agnes," continued Mrs. Stem. "She'll feel slighted if you don't have her."

"Who's that?" demanded Richard from the kitchen.

"Never mind," returned Agnes. "This is my birthday party and I guess I can invite who I please."

"But what have you against her?" reasoned the mother gently.

"Well, who is she anyway? Nothing but an adopted. She doesn't even know where she came from. Tisons found her in a drifting boat out on Blue Lake when they went fishing. She was just a skinny little baby and they took her home and raised her, and adopted her. She thinks she can run around with all us other girls who come from good homes and know who our parents are."

"But she's just as nice a girl as any in your class," put in Richard. His face was flushed, and he fumbled with the jack knife.

"Of course you'd think so," flashed Agnes, "you seem to see something very charming about the young lady."

Richard did not answer, but it wasn't because he couldn't think of anything to say.

"I wish you would march out of the dining room," she continued, "or keep your suggestions to yourself. I want to get these ready to hand out after Sunday school tomorrow."

"And you're honestly not going to invite Annabelle Tison?" Both mother and brother asked the question at the same time.

"I don't intend to," said Agnes positively. "I should think you'd be more particular about my associates. I'm sure if I were her I wouldn't expect to be invited everywhere. I should think she'd prefer to stay at home."

"I'm sorry to hear you talk so, Agnes," spoke Mrs. Stem. "It's the character of your associates I'm particular about. As far as I know she's a good sincere Christian too. I've known for a long time she's only an adopted daughter; in fact, I remember when they found her, but Mrs. Tison loves Annabelle as her own, and Annabelle loves Mrs. Tison as much as any girl loves her mother. She's helpful and obedient, and who knows but what her parents were fine people, finer than the Tisons? At least we must give Annabelle credit for being what she is."

"I'll say," broke in Richard. "She's the prettiest girl in—"

"Keep still there," snapped Agnes. "You can invite her to your birthday party if you like."

No one ate very much at the evening meal. Richard gulped down a few bites and asked to be excused. Mrs. Stem drank two cups of coffee and munched on part of a cinnamon roll. No one touched the creamed sweet potatoes, nor the sliced veal, and they looked so delicious. Agnes said the bread was too brown, and the cherries were too sour, and she didn't like to add sugar to her fruit, so she let them stand.

Mrs. Stem looked hurt and disturbed. She and Mrs. Tison had been fast friends for years. But for greater reason than that, she wiped away some tears as she washed the dishes alone. She went to her bedroom unusually early and called Mr. Stem. It was unusually late before they went to sleep.

Annabelle Tison did not understand at first what all the whispering was about after Sunday school, the next day. Before evening, however, she learned that Agnes Stem was giving a birthday party the next Thursday in honor of her eighteenth birthday, and had given out hand-tinted invitations to all the other girls in the class, and to several of the boys. She was also very conscious of the fact that she had not received one herself.

**

"What is it Annabelle?" The girl's mother looked up from the paper she had been trying to read after church that evening. Something was troubling Annabelle, she felt sure, but it was not the girl's way to express her troubles so quickly.

"Oh, nothing, Mother." But the girl's voice was unsteady and she turned her face to the wall.

"Come, dear, there's something wrong. Don't you feel well today? You worked too long in the attic yesterday."

"No, I didn't Mother. I'm all right. I just can't understand some things."

"None of us can, Annabelle. Did I hurt your feelings or misunderstand you?"

"Oh no, Mother, no, no. You've never done that. I just don't know what Agnes Stem has against me lately. Seems like she treats me colder all the time now—now—" The girl could not finish her sentence for the lump that rose in her throat.

"Don't, honey—it hurts me too, but I don't know why she should treat you so coldly."

"She's having a birthday party on Thursday and I'm the only one in the class who has not been invited,"

"No!"

"Yes Mother, I—I—" Annabelle covered her face with her handkerchief and cried softly. "I don't know what I've ever done against her. Maybe they hate me because I'm—I'm—adopted, you know. I heard them whispering something about it once in the cloak room and they didn't know I was standing close and—"

"Annabelle, it's all right." Her mother's voice was so sweet and tender. "You're just as dear to me and—come over here and lay your head on my shoulder. We'll pray about it tonight,"

"Oh, Mother, I wish I didn't care so, but—but—I do; I mean because I'm not invited."

**

Thursday dawned bright and fair. The sky was clear and blue, and a warm wind played with the children outside. They ran and laughed and skipped like happy squirrels on a sunny day. It was just the kind of a day Agnes hoped it would be. The house was swept and dusted, the porches were scrubbed, the cake was baked, and the ice cream was ready to be frozen. Of course several harsh words had been handed out to her mother in a rush of the morning's tasks, but that was nothing unusual. Some mothers are just naturally provoking, you know! And of all the days in the year, a girl should have no crosses in her path on her birthday! If folks could only realize how important one's eighteenth birthday is!

And it was even more important than Agnes imagined. It was more than cake and ice cream, games and admiring young friends who would each bring a present she could hardly wait to see.

Agnes did most of the talking at the noon meal. Mr. and Mrs. Stem exchanged glances Agnes could not understand. It made her inquisitive at first, then perplexed. They were such, strange, sympathetic, compassionate glances, somehow apart from things of this world, and now and then their eyes were moist.

"Agnes," spoke her father at last in a gentle, faltering voice, as he drew his watch from his pocket. "It is one-fifteen. You may go up to your room and close the door. Here is a key," and he drew from his inside vest pocket, an old rusty key on a bit of red string, and handed it to the girl. "And at one twenty-three, you may unlock the object which is standing in the center of your room. It would not have been our way, but you will soon understand."

"What in the world?" asked Agnes quickly as she held out her hand for the key. She wanted to laugh, but it didn't come.

"Ask no more questions, Agnes, but go up and do as I told you."

An uncanny feeling she could not explain seized Agnes, as she started up the stairs. She had half a notion to ask her mother to go along. Her mother had gone into the bedroom and had closed the door.

At the head of the stairs, Agnes came to an abrupt stop, while a baffled look crossed her face. In the center of her room was a small old-fashioned trunk. She looked at her watch and at exactly one-twenty-three she knelt before the trunk. Very cautiously and with a strange wondering, she turned the rusted lock. The lid cracked and creaked as she tilted it back on it hinges. A more intensely baffled look grew on her face as she started at its contents. On top was a white silk dress, yellow with age, and beside it the picture of a young woman holding a tiny baby. In the other corner on top of an old fashioned shawl, lay a letter on which was written, To Agnes Ilene, my Darling, to be opened on her eighteenth birthday." With nervous fingers, Agnes tore open the envelope and read:

Penndale Hospital
January 4, 1911

My only child, Agnes Ilene,

The doctors say I have but a few days to live, and I must leave you, little one. A kind woman, who found me here and told me the Gospel story, has promised to adopt you and care for you as her own, so I can die in peace. I was a wicked woman and your father died a drunkard, but praise God, this woman who will soon be your mother, has led me to Christ, and I will soon be with Jesus. I want her to take you, because I know she will teach you to love the Lord while you are little. Then you will come to me, my little Agnes, come to be with me in heaven. Oh, it must be beautiful there!

Last night I dreamed I saw angels and heard them singing. You are not very strong, little one, but your eyes are big and bright and your smile is the sweetest I ever saw. This good woman will help you grow strong. Oh, she has been so kind to me. Be obedient to her and love her for all this, little one of mine. She is packing our things and mine in my trunk to give to you when you are eighteen.

You are not quite one now. It is my request that no one look inside the trunk until you do, on your eighteenth birthday. It is my request that you don't know you are adopted until you are old enough to appreciate what your foster parents have done for you. I want nothing to hinder your being a beautiful, pure Christian woman.

My hands shake so I can't write long any more. Mrs. Stern will tell you what else you want to know. God bless her, and God bless you, my little lamb. Soon I will kiss you for the last time. Kiss the good mother often for me. Remember that I die loving you, so love others for me. Read often from the little Bible in the trunk. It is almost like new. Be a good girl, Agnes, my darling. You are to open the trunk at the hour of my departure.

Your mother,
Barbara Lee Tomkin

Agnes swayed with sickness of soul and fell on her knees beside her bed. It was some time before she arose. As in a dream she groped her way to the open trunk and picked up the picture of her mother—her mother.

Oh mystery, incomprehensible, life and death, what eternity of wonder, of grief and love, filled with tears of joy and pain it brings! God in heaven, oh, all wise Father, omniscient and omnipotent are Thy ways. Young hearts are tender and so is God. Agnes wept; but so did Jesus long ago. Her heart was broken, torn and crushed; but so was His—hers for her own sins; His for our sins.

Agnes unfolded the wedding dress carefully. It was handmade and trimmed in rhinestones and lace. The shawl was large and bordered with deep fringe. On it was a slip, "Your grandmother's shawl." Under this was an ivory comb and mirror, and in a tiny box was a cheap gold watch with the name "Barbara" on the back. In the bottom of the little trunk was a beautiful white quilt.

It was three o'clock when Agnes locked the trunk and went down stairs. Her face was white and her eyes were swollen. She found her mother by the bay widow, sewing the snaps on the dress that she intended on wearing that evening.

"Mother," Agnes's voice was almost pitiful, "Mother, I love you. I never—never knew what all you've done for me. I—Oh—"

In a moment they were in each others' arms, Agnes with her head on her mother's breast like a little child. The talked in between their sobs in the sweetest language of love.

"I'm going to put on my wraps now, Mother, and go over to Annabelle's. If she can't forgive me, I won't have the party tonight."

A Message From Blind Eyes

By Carol Hostetler Kauffman, age 28, Hesston, Kansas
Originally published May 4 and 11, 1930,
in the Youth's Christian Companion

Sherman Parker was selling "Quick O Lik" floor mops, dusters and brooms; but even the art of disposing of such mean and homely articles as dirt collectors in exchange for money, requires considerable amount of tact and persuasion with good portion of friendliness mixed in. Sherman thought so, too, after canvassing the north side of Poplar Street, and by the middle of the afternoon, he was convinced of it. He was mistaken when he thought every housewife in town would be anxious to see a demonstration of this new feature.

But with buoyant steps and real enthusiasm he said, "Good afternoon," to the motherly looking woman, who had invited him to step inside her kitchen, and to go ahead with his demonstration while she finished her doughnuts, and who had given him the order that buoyed his spirits up. If only more women were equally as hospitable and obliging!

With a hum in his throat, Sherman turned the corner and rapped at the first door on Sully Avenue, a small red brick house, set well back from the street and if trying to hide its weather-worn face from the gaze of passer-by. A little old lady in a black dress and white cap and apron answered the knock.

"How do you do?" She spoke rather hesitantly, but strangely sweet. She drew a small old-fashioned fascinator closely around her bent shoulders.

"Pardon me, but if I may step inside the wind will not strike you."

"Do that please," spoke the old lady, stepping aside. "I have to be careful these changeable April days that I don't get it in my lungs." Slowly and carefully she measured her way to a rocker close by the stove.

With a glance the young man took in the room. Everything gave the impression of humility, order, and comfortable friendliness. Even the dog on the homemade rug by the table seemed to extend a hearty welcome to this stranger.

Heretofore he had taken little heed to the woman, other than that she was old and small, and slightly bent, but now as he looked at her, there was something that held his attention; he knew not what, unless it was the quaint little cap she wore on her head, or her prim little apron, or maybe her face—ah yes, her face—the eyes! As though a faded, misty, gray veil she looked toward him.

"Well, we've been having nice weather the last few days." Sherman hung his hat on the back of the chair and drew up his outfit kit.

"Very nice," answered the woman, as she loosened the fascinator a little.

"I am representing the Quick O Lik Utility Co. of Dayton, and I am sure you will be as much interested in seeing what we have to of-fer as thousands of other housewives are." Sherman's fastened mop number one on the detachable handle with deft fingers and stepped beside the woman's chair.

"The Quick O Lik people have been working for many years with household cleaning appliances, making a specialty of floor mops and brooms, but this mop is the best and newest thing on the market today, making cleaning a pleasure and much more thorough. You see these section valves, at either end of—"

"I'm sorry, sir," spoke the old woman, "but—you see—I couldn't see to use it, so really you needn't mind about telling me all about it, because I couldn't afford—"

"That's perfectly all right. You are not under any obligation to buy, but—blind, you say?" Sherman's voice sounded almost misgiv-ing. He stood facing the woman with a penetrating stare. Her head rested on one slender hand, but was slightly uplifted toward a canary by the window. He was twittering very softly. It was not difficult now for Sherman to see that the eyes were more than faded and misty, that the rays of day had deepened into night, but instead of making the face dead and shadowy, it shone like a dewy lawn in early morning moonlight. Strange the young man had not noticed it before, but something about the woman's face, too.

"Yes, I've been blind for nearly three years."

"And you—" with wide eyes the young man searched the three small rooms open to his view, "you live here alone?"

"Yes, in a way." Her voice was almost cherry, and a delicate smile lurked about her mouth. "The neighbors are so good to me. They come in and do my cleaning, and do my washing and ironing, and make the fire, and more than I deserve; and then you see, I have a bird." Just then the little yellow creature hopped to the edge of the cage and sang till his breast vibrated in one long spasm. "And my Bible, and oh, a host of pleasant memories and so many friends. Yes, I live alone here in my little home, but you know, the Lord promised never to leave us alone. I presume from your voice that you are quite a young man."

"I'm not twenty yet,"

"So? I've wished more than once I was in my teens again, and could live a few years of my life over. When I was your age, I was one of the vainest girls that walked the streets of Lakeville."

"Lakeville, Minnesota?"

"Yes, have you ever been there?"

"We lived there two years."

"You don't say!" With keen interest the old woman bent forward in her rocker. "We moved up here in 1916."

"Well, we weren't there then yet. Went there from Iowa and came here last spring."

"You're the first person I've met for a long time from Lakeville. We lived in that stone house on the west side of Benton Street. I suppose you've often noticed that place with the three gables."

"Have I? That's exactly where we lived."

"No! We sold that place to a man by the name of Shirley."

"Well, we rented it from him. He built a new home on the corner at the end of the street."

"How time does change things. We moved into that stone house shortly after we were married and lived there for over thirty years, lived and played, laughed and cried there. You're young and life is all ahead of you. You can't imagine being married for forty-five years, I guess."

"I can't imagine being married at all."

The old woman chuckled softly, and rocked a little.

"Well, when I was your age, I thought more of myself than any-thing or anyone else. But there came a time in my life when I saw things different. Do you know, I believe, I'm blind today because—because I was so proud in my young life."

The old woman hung her head a moment, then lifted it and smiled. "I'm not complaining because it's been a real blessing to me; but I wish I could impress young people today how horrible, how re-pulsive, how absolutely sinful it is in the sight of God to be proud."

The color rose in the young man's face, and he was glad the wom-an could not see it. He cleared his throat and shifted from one foot to the other. He almost wished he had not invited himself into the house, yet there was a power that held him and made him anxious to hear more. Without realizing it, he sat down and searched the woman's face. Without a doubt she had been a pretty girl, for her eyes, though sightless were still large and heavily lashed and the hair, though nearly white, was still thick and fell in gentle waves around her temples.

"I'm happy today, oh, so happy, even though Harvey had to go a year ago and leave me here alone without almost nothing. We were always happy, after—after the thing happened that changed my life. It happened the third year we were married. But maybe you're in a hurry?"

"No—no—go ahead." The young man bent forward a trifle and watched the many expressions that crossed the woman's face while she spoke. He did not notice that the leaves on the trees outside were turning up, and off into the north a treacherous cloud was gathering.

"I don't tell my experiences often, but somehow, I feel like telling you. If you're a Christian it won't hurt you, and if you're not it won't hurt you either."

The man did not answer.

**

"I always had a hankering after pretty things no matter what they cost. I couldn't be satisfied with just common things and I spent Harvey's money faster than he made it. I was determined to have a fur coat and a real one too. Harvey never liked fur coats, but I did because they weren't as common then as they are now. Harvey said he'd get me anything I needed, but he just couldn't convince himself of the fact that I needed a fur coat. We had some words about it, but they were mostly my words. I always knew when Harvey had little to say, he was doing a lot of thinking. Well, to make my story short, I sneaked money out of my household allowance for over two years and hid it. Harvey, of course could not understand where all the money went to, but I explained that as best I could and nothing more was said. I had $265.00 saved up, enough for a down payment on a coat. I didn't worry about the rest. I looked over the coats and picked out the one I wanted—a beautiful thing—genuine squirrel (at least they had me believe it) for only $825.00. I'd step pretty in that; I thought I'd have all my friends casting jealous eyes at me. I had the money in small steel strong-box and hid it in the basement in a broken place in the cement wall, right beside the water pipe that comes in from the outside."

Sherman sat erect and for a few seconds stopped breathing.

"I started to town about two o'clock with the intention of having the coat fitted and altered slightly, then go down again after supper with Harvey and take the money along—surprise him, you know, and get the coat. On the way to town, I was knocked down by a four-horse-omnibus, which dashed around the corner as I was crossing Arcade Avenue. I was in the hospital nearly three months, and oh, how I suffered! They never expected me to live the first week, and I thought part of the time I was dead, and when I knew I wasn't, I hoped I would be. Oh, it was a terrible feeling. I can't describe it. Worst of all, I thought if I ever did get well, I would never be fit to look at. There are no scars on my face that you can see, but I must have been a sight at first. They never allowed me to look at myself for weeks. My nose was smashed flat to my face, my head cut, my shoulder broken and the nerves to my eyes stunned. I've had trouble with my eyes ever since that, and finally went blind, you see.

It was starting to rain, but neither was aware of it.

"But, this is not half so bad as the terrible blindness of heart that I had. No, never! In my half-conscious state, I saw all my friends walking past me in fur coats, laughing at me in my rags. I saw my heart torn out, hanging before me black and shriveled. I thought I was hiding money in every conceivable crack and crevice in the cellar wall and couldn't pull or dig it out again. Harvey said I talked about hiding money all that first week, told him to go and get it, but he thought I was out of my head and paid no attention to it.

"When I finally awoke out of that delirium, Harvey was there praying beside my bed and talking to me so kindly about how much God loved me, and about summer time and trees and brooks and music, till my mind got clear again. Oh, Harvey, he was a real Christian; the golden rule kind. I had the experience he had till—till then. I had our minister come to the hospital and I confessed my sins. Oh, I needn't relate all that, but, oh, the joy that came into my soul, I'll never forget and it made Harvey so happy, too. He cried like a child, but oh, such a sweet cry it was. After the minister went, I confessed to Harvey how I had skimped for a fur coat and never had any to start our saving account. I told him where I had hid that $265.00. 'Are you sure you are talking in your right mind, Lydia?' He said. 'Why, Harvey, don't I look like it? It's true. Go home and look. It's there beside that water pipe back behind the furnace there in the dark. I doesn't show, but with a light you'll see it.'

"Well, Harvey came in the next day and talked to the nurse a long time before he came into my room, and as soon as he came in, of course, I asked if he found the money. He said the nurse said he shouldn't talk about anything that would excite me, but that made me all the more excited, till Harvey had to tell me."

The young man shifted uneasily in his chair. It was raining quite fast now. He took no heed.

"He said that water pipe sprung a leak the day after I was hurt, and the plumber was out to fix it and put in a new elbow and plastered up the wall. I don't need to describe how I fainted and got a backset, and all that. But that plumber took that money. It was right there and he couldn't have helped seeing it. Harvey went and talked to the man, but of course he denied it. That was no more than was to be expected. He has been found out before for stealing. Harvey went to his boss. He wouldn't have him arrested, but the man lost his job, and about the same time got a new home, so it is evident he got the money. That's all past and gone these forty years. We were three years paying our doctor bill, but it took that experience to make me happy and content with what we could afford. I suffered more after that than ever before, and I never got a fur coat, either!"

A smile almost angelic crossed the old woman's face as she rested her head on the back of her chair.

"Yes—" her voice was almost a whisper, "yes, life is strange, and the world has little to offer, but is ready to deprive; but I've got something that all the world—no ten worlds could never rob me of—"

Under her breath the old woman whispered something. It might have been a prayer.

Sherman Rogers pulled out his handkerchief and wiped his forehead. The day wasn't hot.

"It sounds like it's raining."

"Yes," Sherman's voice was husky. He cleared his throat. "It started to rain a little while ago."

"I am sorry—perhaps I should have not taken so much of your time when I didn't buy anything, but when you said you lived in Lakeville and in our old home seemed like I almost lived back there again for a while."

"Your story was interesting; I'm sure, and—very unusual. Since it's raining, I believe I'll strike home."

He gathered up his outfit, not with the deft fingers he had undone it, but awkwardly, nervously, as though he had done a hard day's work, and was utterly fatigued. And glib as he usually was of tongue, for the life of him, he couldn't think of a thing to say. Then the woman spoke.

"You haven't told me whether you are a Christian." The old woman's voice was very tender.

"I—a—," Sherman clicked the latch oh his kit and picked up his hat. "I can't say that I've had such an experience to be sure, but I hope I'm a Christian. I was taken into the church several years ago, but—"

"But you're not satisfied, is that it? Did you tell me your name? I forgot."

"I don't believe I did. Rogers is my name, Sherman Rogers—and yours?"

"Martin is my name. It's not a hard name to remember, but it's not necessary to remember the name, but remember this: I'm going to start praying for you till you find the peace you want. There's not much I can do; but I can pray. God has wonderful promises for those who believe in prayer. Young folks now-a-days don't seem to care a lot about old people, but I care a lot about them, and I have more young folks on my list, than old people. I wish you success not only in your Christian life, but in your business as well, Mr. Rogers."

"Thank you, Mrs. Martin, and thank you for your interest in a stranger. Good-day."

**

Sherman's clothes were soaked when he returned home. About seven o'clock, he called up a chum and told him he would be unable to go along with him to the social.

There are some experiences in every life that may be lived over again and again, in one evening. There are places, houses, object, moments that loom up before one, causing the original emotions to surge through a person's body. This is not only true of sinful experiences, but of triumphant and victorious experiences as well. The past is sometimes more vivid than the present.

At about eleven o'clock, Sherman was still sitting at the table in his room, when his head dropped on his arm, under which lay an open Bible and a checkbook.

Heaven blessed the next day with a beautiful sky above and a budding, blossoming earth beneath. Every bursting bud on every tree seemed to tremble and laugh for joy. Mrs. Martin was humming softly, when someone knocked at the front door.

"Come" she called.

"Good morning, Mrs. Martin."

"Oh, it's the mop man! Good morning. I recognized your voice at once. But really, I didn't expect to hear it so soon again."

"You said yesterday that life was strange and maybe you'll think so when I hand you this."

Sherman drew from his billfold, a yellow paper and placed it in her hand. His breath came in quick gasps and his hands trembled.

"It is a check for $265.00."

"A check for—" she nearly dropped the paper.

"Yes, Mrs. Martin, a check. I didn't steal that money. I wasn't in the world then yet, but I found that money while we were living in that house."

"Found! Found it! Not stolen? It never can—"

"It's true, Mrs. Martin. I'll tell you just how it happened. That same pipe sprang a leak one morning and the landlord sent a plumber out and when I got home from school at noon I went down to the cellar to investigate. The plumber had gone home for dinner, but he had the wall knocked out around there for about a foot. When I was poking around in there thinking I might discover the retreat of a rat I had seen about the house, I saw a corner of something in a little pocket hole, just back of the wall. I dug it out, and there was a little steal box, rusted and crusty. I pried it open with a screw driver—I gasped—I ran upstairs. The folks thought I had gone mad; then we all went mad for a little. I said, it's mine! It's mine! Finally father said, 'You can keep it, but you can't spend a cent of it, till you're of age.' None outside my parents ever heard about it. Father wanted to tell the landlord, but Mother and I said 'No.'

"That was in March, three years ago. I found that box, and every day since, I've lived in a dream of what I was going to do with that money when I reached twenty-one. They changed, of course, but every chance I had, I added to that. That's why I am selling mops now. I was going to get a car—pay cash—have my friends cast jealous eyes at me—as—as you said yesterday. I've dreamed car, every night, but now—oh, Mrs. Martin, I've been too proud about it."

He was glad she could not see his lips trembling and the glistening tear that fell on his coat sleeve. Boy's seldom shed tears; but when people can't see, and they just crowd themselves out, it's not so bad. Mrs. Martin said nothing, but tears came to her faded eyes and burned them sharply.

"Boys don't care so much for clothes as girls do, but there's a lot of other things we take pride in. Father doesn't want me to get a car of my own as long as I run with the bunch I do. But I can't now—I won't need any."

"God moves in a mysterious way, His wonders to perform. I—I can't comprehend it yet. This—this paper is—"

"Yes, it's good, Mrs. Martin. I'll take it down and deposit it for you if you want me to. Anything I might do wouldn't mean what you've meant to me already."

"Oh, would to God I could see the face of such a man!"

"No, Mrs. Martin, I'm only beginning to be a man."

A Peek into Dale's Diary

Something New and Different You'll Enjoy

By Carol Hostetler Kauffman, age 28, Hesston, Kansas
Originally published July 20, 1930, in the
Youth's Christian Companion

Well, one of the things I said I would never do was to keep a diary, but since Aunt Fanny gave it to me for my birthday, Ma says I ought to show my appreciation and use it. I don't see any use in it, and, anyway, I always thought they were for girls. I hope none of the fellows ever find out I started this. It rained today, meaning I had to put the papers clear up to the doors, and I was almost late for supper, and Ma had strawberry short cake.

June 4

It didn't rain today but it tried to awful hard. Us fellows went fishing below the dam, and I caught none, so we watched the machine shovel for about an hour. They'll start paving next week, then we'll go fishing again. Ma says, when a boy is thirteen, he ought to know enough to go home for supper on time, especially when company's coming. Flemings were here and Ma nearly burned the biscuits because I was ten minutes late. Their little girl cried most of the time, and the folks talked about the new preacher that is coming.

June 5

Samsey's house caught on fire this morning, and I was the first one there. The firemen had it out in a minute, and it wasn't near as exciting as I hoped it would be. I had to take back everything I carried out. If the fireman would have been a minute later, it would have been exciting. I had to hoe the garden and Ma said I hoed out some of her sweet corn, and she told Dad. I don't see why she has to tell Dad everything. I didn't get to go swimming.

June 6

Ma said a boy my age ought to find a job, but Dad said not 'til after Summer Bible School is over. Us fellows sure had fun with Mrs. Ward last summer. She couldn't do a thing with us, and she never found out yet who stuck the chicken feather in her bonnet and erased the map of Palestine and brought the toad to school. How the girls did scream. I found a new place to hide this diary so Martha can't find it. Sisters are supposed to make their brother's beds and go right out, but I'll vouch they don't.

June 7

I had to mow the lawn and wash the car this morning so I could go swimming this afternoon. Tige can dive the best, and next comes me. Sam can't do anything but tag along. On the way home we took the rent sign out of Bank's empty house and tacked it on a bird house across the street and put a private-drive sign in the window, and put a detour sign in old Mrs. Taylor's yard over her keep-off-the-grass warning, and some more things. We sure had fun. Ma had banana cream pie for supper and I ate two pieces.

June 8

We were invited to Menges for dinner which was very good, all but the salad. Some funny mixture Martha went daffy over. They talked about almost everything. The new preacher looks pretty good. He looks a lot younger than Dad and I like the way he walks. His name is Berman.

June 9

Summer Bible School started today and Mr. Berman is our teacher. I don't know if I'll like him or not. He has a stern look and sees everything that goes on. Mrs. Ward has one of the primary classes.

I started to read Toney's Adventures today and it is great. I had two flat tires on my bike tonight. I was late for supper again but I got two new customers, so Ma didn't scold me.

June 11

Us fellows can't get much over Mr. Berman. I tried to imitate a little chicken in school today and he caught me the first time, and he had his back turned. George tried it once and he caught him and made us stay after school. But he never said a word about that. He asked us to help typo graph some maps and things. He doesn't seem like the other preachers. I don't know what he seems like. He can sing bass or tenor. I'm going to sing bass.

June 12

I'm too tired to write much and I've got to get up early and read over the fifth chapter of Matthew and do some other things. Mr. Berman knows everything about birds and snakes and trees and rocks, and he can yodel. I'm going to learn how. Lloyd Platt almost got his leg broke.

June 13

Tilson broke a window in the church today, but his mother didn't have any money so Mr. Berman said if Till could repeat the sixth chapter of Matthew tomorrow, he would stand good for it. I think it will cost about four dollars. Us fellows went down to watch them pave this afternoon and we saw a wreck on Woodland Ave. Two ladies were hurt and I didn't get my papers till 2:20. Martha had a bunch of girls here tonight and they did a lot of giggling and jabbering and pieced a quilt or something for Grandma Suton. Ma served cake and ice cream so I stayed in the kitchen with Dad.

June 14

Nothing happened today but I had a tooth filled. I'm never going to be a dentist. They think they have the right to hurt a fellow as much as they please. Ma made me go.

June 15

Mr. Berman talked to the juniors today about people in the hills of Virginia. It was better than Toney's Adventures. Six of us fellows helped him pass out tracts this afternoon, and then we gathered wild flowers in Slaber's Grove and took them to old man Trousen. The doctor said he can't live two weeks and we had prayer for him. Mr. Berman can pray the best I ever heard. It makes me feel funny like.

June 16

I caught three pigeons this morning so we had pot pie for dinner. I made good recitations in school today, but it was too hot to do much else, so I slept under the apple tree all afternoon.

June 18

It rained all day so we couldn't go outside for recess. It's more fun inside anyway. Mr. Berman had us sit on the floor in the basement, and we played Bible-character guessing game, then he told us about John C. Patton. I hope it rains tomorrow so he can tell the rest. I got three new customers today and lost one for two months. Smiths are going to California. I'd rather go to Africa.

June 19

It didn't rain after all today. It doesn't seem to rain enough this summer. I made the best map on the blackboard today, and poorest grade in music. Ma said she thinks I'll never sing any better than Dad, but I know I can.

June 20

Something terrible happened today. It wasn't so bad, but Martha thought it was terrible. Her canary got out some way and the cat got to it. She cried all day almost and Ma said she would get her another one. A man was here trying to sell Dad a new car which I wish he would, but Dad said not as long as our brothers in Russia need our help. He gave quite a bit already, but I don't know how much.

June 21

This was a fine day. I was busy all day. Uncle Ben came tonight.

June 22

I like Uncle Ben. He knows the most things. Next to Mr. Berman I think, Uncle Ben is the best man I know. He has the jolliest laugh and bends over and shakes like a dish of Jell-O. He can preach, too, next to Mr. Berman. He talked to me on the porch while Ma was getting dinner.

June 23

The Bible School goes so fast this summer. I wish it would last all summer. We are going to have an outing Saturday.

June 24

I never knew before that Jesus was such a man. Mr. Berman must be something like Him. I am going to read a book he gave me now. We put our work on the walls today for exhibit.

June 25

The parents visited the school today and we had our picture taken. I don't think it will be very good because I was just starting to put down Clyde's hand from his face and John was spitting out his gum.

June 26

Mr. Berman said I ought to take penmanship so I could learn to write nicer. We almost had a cyclone today and it tore half of our maple tree down and broke two windows. We can't use our telephone yet. I read some more in the book tonight.

June 27

We had Children's Church today. Mr. Berman preached to us and asked how may wanted to be Christians. I stood up and so did five other fellows and Martha and Lucy and Anna. After school I told

Mrs. Ward those tricks I did and she said I should forget it and live a new life. I'm going to walk down toward the swimming pool tomorrow and see if those signs are straight.

June 28

The more I think of it the more I want to be a missionary. I wish Mr. Berman wasn't so much older than I am and we could go together. Mr. Berman is coming here for dinner tomorrow. I wish no one else would be here but us two.

A Simple Picture

By Carol Hostetler Kauffman, age 28, Hesston, Kansas
Originally published August 31, 1930,
in the Youth's Christian Companion

The east-bound Oriental Limited roared through the night over shining rail, past golden wheat fields like a blazing arrow. It was a pleasant summer night, and in one of the coaches sat a young man idly watching the strangers around him. Several times he lifted his position restlessly or peered through the gathering night at the blurred, flying landscape.

At a glance one would judge the young man to be of exceptionally fine character. The general outline of his face showed him to be a man of determination and pluck, yet there was no limit to his roughness. He was well dressed, but not according to dictates of the clothier of the day.

He looked again over the front page of the Minneapolis Tribune, and laid it beside him mechanically. A tiny speck of white, the corner of something in the crevice of the red plush cushioned seat, caught his eye, and as mechanically as he had discarded the evening paper, he drew out the—but instead of finding what he supposed to be a card, he looked straight into the pleasant, half smiling, half plaintive face of a girl. Neil Godfrey frowned slightly, and then stared in dumb bewilderment. Once he almost laughed, and was about to stick it back in its hiding place, but something withheld his hand.

The girl had on a white dress that fell in soft folds around her slender ankles, and she was standing in front of a blossoming dogwood tree. That was all. There was nothing about the picture that would leave the impression she was of high birth or low, her face was intelligent and expressive, her dress neat and dainty, and her position stately, but not haughty. For half an hour he studied her.

Neil wondered at himself that an ordinary picture could claim his undivided attention so long. In fact he was almost disgusted that he was allowing this unknown girl to trouble his thoughts, when instead of entertaining a new puzzle, or spending the entire evening on the day's news, or watching the people leaving and entering the train; he should be going over his conference speech.

The annual Iowa-Nebraska Conference was scheduled to open session the following day. Neil Godfrey was assigned the subject of "Simplicity," under the topic of "Young Peoples' Problems," to be discussed the second day. His outline had been definitely decided upon the week before, and two days before leaving home, all the minor points had been filled in. He had spent hours of conscientious study on the subject, and yet he intended to go over it once more on the train, fasten his points, arouse a greater enthusiasm, and readjust a few statements.

Nevertheless, the first hundred miles of a train ride, after a morning of hard work in the field, is not particularly conducive to sound thinking, especially when the little girl across the aisle is tormenting her mother most of the time for ice cream cones or candy, and when half a dozen giddy high school girls just ahead are trying to entertain the entire coach.

Neil still held the picture in his hand. He seemed to have forgotten the laughter and the silly performances ahead. Even the child's shines at the side made no effect on him. The expression on the face seemed to change slightly as the light fell on it from different angles. There was something about the face which invited his confidence. It seemed to sympathize, understand, and encourage. Without knowing why, that face seemed to breathe a divine fire within the young man which animated his whole being with desire to be better than he had ever been before, to forget the failures he had made, and hope harder, and strive more faithfully. He looked, and the lips seemed to part slightly into a pleasant smile. They seemed almost to speak.

"I wonder how her voice sounds?" he said to himself. "Old-fashioned, I suppose, like the rest of her."

Just then it occurred to Neil for the first time that her dress was not of the present vogue, though of fashionable length, for the sleeves were gathered at the top and the hemline was decidedly even.

"Oh, mysterious being," he whispered. "Who are you? You look like a woman, but your face is so young, and innocent, so pure, so, so simple. That's it!"

From the brief-case at his right, Neil Godfrey drew out his notebook and jotted something down. Without any difficulty, he went over his speech. A new vigor and earnestness spurred him on. An unseen Spirit dominated every thought. He prayed. He closed his notebook, put the picture in his inside coat pocket and lay back in his seat for the night.

Neil had nearly finished his speech. The audience had given him splendid attention and even though the day was hot, they forgot to use their fans. People were leaning forward in their seats. Now and then, a hearty "Amen" was given by some of the older men.

"True simplicity is a jewel rarely found," continued Neil. "In character, in manner, in style, in supreme excellence of beauty, is simplicity. I had rather a unique coincidence on my trip down here, day before yesterday. I found a picture of a young woman. Someone evidently lost a treasure, for she is someone's daughter or sweetheart or sister. I was surprised to find such a picture in a public place where all about me seemed saturated with pride and affection, for the longer I looked at that picture, the more it portrayed what I have been trying to say. She was the very picture of simplicity such as I would wish a sister of mine if I had one. It would help to solve the problems of young people, especially the young men, if our country, yes our church, had more simple, humble, and truehearted young women." Another "Amen" was heard and Neil took his seat.

During the lunch hour that evening someone touched Neil on the shoulder, "Mr. Godfrey?" Neil turned and took the outstretched hand. "Hager is my name," said the tall friendly chap.

"I'm glad to meet you," said Neil.

"Do you happen to have that picture with you, you spoke of this afternoon?"

"Yes," answered Neil with surprise. And he drew it from his inside pocket. The other took it with an utterance of joy.

"I've carried this picture in my Bible for ten years, but I didn't know where I lost it. I remember I had it on the train Tuesday and I moved up a coach to get away from those silly high school girls, and that evening, I missed it."

"Your—your lady friend?" stammered Neil blushing slightly.

"Yes, my mother." Bert Hager noticed the look of astonishment and went on.

"I never remembered her. She died when I was about two, and father gave me this picture when I was eight and I've carried it with me ever since. I've worked for her, lived for her. I'll do anything to please her. She's meant to me what you said today and more. She speaks to me, she loves me, as not everyone else does." Bert's voice was a little unsteady. He put the picture in his inside coat pocket, tenderly, carefully, as though it might crumble or break.

"I thank you a thousand times. Strange you got that same seat."

"Stranger yet, that I noticed it, and stranger still that we met in this way. That picture has helped me more than I can tell. I never knew my mother either, and I never saw a picture of her."

"Your father must have one somewhere."

"I never saw it if he has. My step-mother is all right, but she can't understand a fellow like your own. Let me look at her once more. Where are you going for the night?" asked Neil after a moment.

"I don't know yet," said Bert.

"Let's go to the same place if you don't mind. I have some problems I'd like to talk over with you. I believe we could understand each other."

"Good," said Bert. They walked to the ticket stand together.

"Your home?" asked Neil

"Benton, Montana. And yours?"

"Blue River, Washington, and we came on the same train and only found it out? Strange isn't it?"

And in the years to come each discovered many things in the other, which helped them solve their peculiar problems, for the prayers of the mothers now in heaven, welded a true and lasting friendship between their boys they left behind.

The Angel's Charge

By Carol Hostetler Kauffman, age 28, Hesston, Kansas
Originally published September 30, 1930,
in the Youth's Christian Companion

A small green-shaped lamp on the dressing table cast a soft cool light over the bedroom, revealing an indistinct form under the white covers. A girl of about fourteen summers, lay sleeping. But the moist hair clinging to the forehead, the flushed face and the restless movements, showed plainly, she was not sleeping the sleep of perfect health. Several times she groaned, not as if in pain, but in keen expectation.

Now and then a dull thud sent her arms twitching and she half opened her eyes. It may have been the wind bumping the side of the house, or it may have been that a loose board on the top stair-step creaked without walking; the girl turned her head on the pillow.

Mr. and Mrs. Hosmer were spending the week-end with relatives in Guilford. Celia and Gordon were at home alone, that is, until the evening of this story.

Before the two had finished their supper, Gordon's foreman had called to notify him that he was to report for the night shift at eight-fifteen. He went without asking any questions over the phone, for Gordon had learned like most of the other drifters (some too late) that it never profited anything to argue with, or interrogate, their boss. Gordon did nevertheless ask himself a few questions on his way to the factory. And Celia had asked a number of questions Gordon could not answer.

Celia had been completely upset over what had occurred the day before. Gordon had come home from work an hour late. The ice cream Celia had made all herself in the early afternoon was half melted. And she had made it in the new two-quart galvanized freezer she bought on dollar day. The coffee was bitter, because it percolated too long. How proudly she set her evening meals out for them. It was her first experience in cooking and planning the meals all alone. And now to have her brother come home so late, and with such an expression on his face, set her nerves trembling. She always was a nervous, delicate child of a girl.

"What is it Gordon?" asked Celia before he had his cap off.

"Oh—I got myself into trouble, I'm afraid."

"Trouble? What trouble?" Celia's eyes opened wider than ever and her hand went to her throat nervously.

"Oh, Cameron got after me again tonight."

"About what, Gordon, that money for the pool hall?"

"Yeh." Gordon's voice was dry and husky.

"But he can't force any one to contribute a cent, let alone ten dollars—why, it's unreasonable."

"I know it, Celia, but—"

"But didn't you tell him you couldn't conscientiously do it and that we don't patronize such places and—?"

"I've told him everything, Sis, and the more I argue with him the more furious he gets. I left him in a rage tonight. I tell you, Celia, Cameron never stops to argue with anyone. What he says goes, and even Tige Taskie cowers in front of him. The first time he approached me about it, I told him my reasons for refusing and I thought he accepted them, but it's the gang that's heading him on. I'm the only one in the factory who refused. In the mass meeting last Saturday noon, I was the only man who didn't sign the pledge. The men are raving for the hall like hungry tigers for fresh meat. They can't smoke while they work and there's so place but the alley to park in at noon, and they'll gladly give ten dollars. Cameron is going to pay the thousand himself. And on the first of November every man is to get a five cent raise on the hour because he figures this recreation hall will make the men that much more efficient. Oh, its modern psychology, Sis.

"And what did he say, Celia? He called me a—well I don't need to tell you. He threatened to fire me, or deprive me of the raise, and—and he said the other fellows were going to clean up on me. He said even if I wouldn't use the pool room, it was the only sportsmanlike thing to do to help the other men enjoy it. I say, Celia, he was ugly to me, but this is only making you nervous. Come, let's eat—ice cream? Now, Sis, you know just what I like, don't you?"

"Yes, but it's melting, Gordon. It was just right at six o'clock."

"I'll believe that it was, Sis, but I came as soon as I could."

"And he kept you an hour?"

"I suppose I'd be there yet, but I simply stopped arguing with him and let him think he was making me feel cheap. I wish Dad was at home. I don't know what to do. I have a notion to quit, but what else could I do, with two thousand men out of work and Dad has to meet that note. I suppose I'll be asked to quit this morning."

And this is the reason why Gordon asked no questions of Cameron over the phone; and this is the reason why he could not answer Celia's questions, for he had never before been called on duty for the night shift. He had not been home from work more than an hour. They were both secretly alarmed. Gordon tried to hide the fact from his sister, and she had tried to hide it from him. But girls are not so clever as they themselves think.

She walked with him to the edge of the porch. The wind was playing havoc with the loose leaves on the grass and there were no stars in sight.

"You'll go to bed of course?" asked Gordon tenderly.

"Well—I—guess so." In spite of herself Celia's voice shook. "You'll let me know as soon as you're home?"

"Yes." And Gordon was around the corner.

For some time the girl stood where she was, watching the leaves and thinking—thinking. Her brain began to whirl, her body trembled and her face was colorless, and still she stood there.

"What if the gang would clean up on him? What did that mean? Would they—would they, Oh! With a cry of fear and indignation Celia ran into the house and closed the door. The house felt so empty. It was.

As every other evening, so on this one, Celia opened her own little Bible and read, in the order of her consecutive reading, the ninety-first Psalm. With bated breath, she drank in those verses like a hurt child does its milk between sobs. With reverent thankful passion she reread the ancient hymn, and with the Bible clasped open to her breast, she knelt beside her bed, and in simple faith claimed those promises. With a prayer warm on her lips, she fell into unsound sleep.

Carefully the man reconnoitered, then rose and walked stealthily into the house. Three followed suit, and stood in file at the foot of the stairs. The first man climbed the steps, slowly, cautiously. Several times he stopped short and listened from above. The steps creaked mercilessly, much to his disgust. He entered the room first. It was empty. He stopped abruptly at the door of the next room. A strange noise came from the dressing table, the stranger could see it was not the object of his prey, but a girl with face drawn and crimson in an effort to breathe. One arm was tossed above her head, and in the other was clasped a small black Bible. A stifled brassy cough came from the girl, and the man instantly put his hand on the ugly weapon at his side. He stood looking at the girl. It almost seemed to him that she sensed there was someone in the room, but he could not quite rouse herself. Then she breathed easier for a few minutes.

The stranger scanned the room briefly, excitedly. If this was not his prey, why not go? On the wall above the bed hung a hand-painted motto "My heart is fixed on Thee, O Lord."

Another brassy, resonant cough drew the intruder suddenly to a side. The girl opened her eyes, this time, and lifted her head from the pillow, only to let it drop with a sigh—her breathing came harder and faster.

"Gordon" she called feebly. No answer. "Bring him home, Jesus," she whispered.

The man stood breathless, watching, wondering. The girl's chest rattled and she moaned. As in a spasm of pain, she tossed over to her side, her face to the wall, and the man measured his way to the door and slipped from the room unnoticed.

Halfway down the stairs he met one of his companions, and at the foot, the other two. He touched them and motioned them to follow. As one man, they left the house as noiselessly as they had entered, and were off in the car which was waiting at the curb.

"Where's your man?" demanded the driver roughly.

"That's what I'd like to know. The rascal, the coward stepped out. Coward, the beast ran off and left his kid sister home alone, with the whooping cough, or croup, or somethin'.

Kid's 'bout choking to death in her sleep. If I had him we'd clean up on him for that in a bargain."

"Let's hang around till he pulls in."

"Nah, its gettin' light before long. Tomorrows another day."

Half an hour later Celia was awakened by the door bell. She sat up in bed and looked around. Gordon always came right in. She clutched the covers frantically in pain, but before she could gather herself to her feet, a young woman in black garb and cap stood at the door and spoke gently.

"Miss Hosmer, just stay in bed. I came as quickly as I could."

As in a dream, Celia looked at the approaching figure. She tried to speak, but could not.

"You are frightened?" asked the woman.

Still Celia could not answer. The woman felt the girl's head and took her hand.

"You have a treacherous cold, my dear."

"Oh, have I?"

"Where?" and the woman looked around.

"Someone is here with you surely?"

"Why—why—Gordon—No, he is working. Yes, I am alone."

"Who was it that called me out then?"

"Called you out?" Surely Celia was dreaming. She tried to rouse herself. She rubbed her eyes.

"Someone, a gentleman, called some thirty minutes ago, and told me to call as soon as possible 241 Cresley Ave, that Miss Hosmer was very ill and, and he said something I couldn't understand about being alone."

"I—" Celia nearly cried now. "I can't understand. I—I feel so queer. Who are you please?"

"Sister Marie, one of the night deaconesses. But that does not matter, does it dear? Some friend sent me, and now I am here to help you and I will at once."

She took from a bag a bottle and gave her patient a little from a dropper.

"That's not so bad, is it? And now I need hot water and a basin."

"Downstairs, Sister Marie; but I can get them for you."

"No indeed, you shant."

"But, I didn't know I was sick. I—"

"It hurts to talk, Miss Hosmer. Just be quiet please."

For over an hour the deaconess worked with the girl, saying only a word now and then. Oh, her hands were so kind and her voice, so gentle. In strange, wonder, but in child-like-faith Celia fell into a peaceful sleep.

Gordon came home at six. He ran upstairs with a bound, but at the door of Celia's room, he came to an abrupt stop, while an astonished exclamation escaped from his lips.

Beside Celia's bed sat a nurse, with her gaze fixed on the girl's gently breathing form.

"What?" But the Sister motioned for Gordon to be quiet; however she had been too late, for Celia recognized the step and she opened her big gray eyes.

"Did—did you call her out, Gordon?"

"Me? No. Who called her out? Don't you know?" he addressed the sister.

"Some gentleman, sir. He did not give his name, but he seemed to know there was someone sick here, and told me to come out at once; so I did."

"God bless you for it, Sister Marie, and bless the unknown sender too. I—a—this is strange. You were alone, Celia?"

She nodded. "I must have been my guardian angel, for I didn't even realize I was so sick, Gordon."

"Yes, Sis."

"Are you going back to work today?"

"Today? Why honey this is Sunday. No not till tomorrow. And—Cameron told me this morning I can stay on, and needn't bother about the ten dollars.

"He—he did. Oh, Gordon"

"I can't understand it, Celia. He was as nice to me as he could be. Sister Marie come down with me, I want to talk to you, or—are you better, Celia? What is it, a cold?"

"I guess so, but I am better now, but I can't think quite right. Maybe I can if you read the ninety-first Psalm to me."

A happy, surprised look grew on Gordon's face as he read and it never passed away. The men all noticed it on Monday and one man in particular treated Gordon especially kind, although he never felt quite free around him.

Dale's Diary

By *Carol Hostetler Kauffman, age 28, Hesston, Kansas*
Originally published October 12, 1930,
in the Youth's Christian Companion

Sept 8

School started today. They say the eighth grade is easier than the seventh. I will soon find out. I'm sitting in J-9 beside Thetus Parker, behind Lois Cushing. The fellows all tease me about it, but I like Parker, even if he is black. His granddad came from Africa, and I'm going to ask Parkie a bunch of questions. Lois is some girl!

Sept 9

I walked to the corner with Mr. Berman after Prayer Meeting to-night. I like him better every day. He seems to know me better than I do myself. He said I was troubled with doubts again. Funny, how he can tell. He asked me to go stargazing with him tomorrow night.

Sept 10

It's nearly eleven. I'm too happy to write. I'll never let the other fellows know. They'd call me sentimental. I'll do what I promised Berman.

Sept 11

Miss Jones asked Lois today where macaroni comes from. She said Macaroni trees. Yesterday Mr. Peters asked her what the capital of New York was and she said London. Ha. Parkie and I took our lunches down in the furnace room so we could talk and the other fellows wouldn't find us.

Sept 12

Pa asked me last night if I used his razor for anything. I said no. I didn't sleep very much. This morning I put a note in his overall pocket. I wonder if he found it.

Sept 13

I made $3.50 on my papers this week. We took our supper to the South Pine Park tonight and I drank nine cups of iced tea and watched the baby lions till it got dark. After we got home Pa told me he found the note this morning; then we sat on the banister and ate the left over ice cream. Pa was nice to me.

Sept 14

Mr. Berman took five of us fellows along to the jail this afternoon. Wonder how it would seem to be penned up behind those bars for a week or a year? The darkie looked a lot like Parkie. I'm going to ask him if he knows any one in there. I'll have to be careful though. Parkie has a temper. One man started to cry and told Mr. Berman he wanted to talk to him alone. Us fellows all had to go out. I wonder what was the matter? Mr. Berman didn't talk all the way home.

Sept 15

Martha sure writes a lot of letters. I don't see what all the girls can think of to say. The only one I ever wrote was an answer to a puzzle and I never got that fifty yet. I was going to get something useful with it too. I wanted to go out to the airport tonight and Pa said I couldn't. I believe he would have let me but Ma said no first.

Sept 16

Hardly any of us fellows like English. We had to read our own themes out loud today and Miss Bartley said mine was worth 78. Parkie got 62 and Lois got 63. What do fellows know about grass weaving anyway? I like geography and history best.

Sept 17

Parkie doesn't know nearly so much about Africa as I thought he would. He'd rather talk about America. He's going to be a doctor. Sunday afternoon I'm going to watch him operate on a cat. George and Clyde are trying to get acquainted with Parkie now, too.

Sept 18

Pa got Martha a typewriter for her birthday today. She says she's going to be a stenographer. I'm going to learn to write while she's doing the dishes and things so I can be a telegraph operator, if I decide to. Wonder what Pa will get me. I've got about 8 ½ months to wonder.

Sept 19

I'm to give a talk in Y. P. M. Sunday night on "Lessons from the life of Joseph." I went over to have Mr. Berman help me and he wasn't at home so I stopped to see Lloyd on the way back and his big sister gave us watermelon on the back steps. I cared for more but didn't get it. I heard Lloyd's Pa and another man talking in the kitchen about something. I'm going to find out. Sounded awful suspicious.

Sept 20

Parkie didn't do his stunt today. I never saw him. Tommy Druber fell out of the swing when it was going high and he got his skull fractured. Ma was over there all day and Martha did the baking which doesn't taste like Ma's. Tommy is the cutest chap in the neighborhood.

Sept 21

They took Tommy to the hospital and had special prayer. It stormed and tore up things tonight. Martha came into my room and almost saw this journal! I'd rather burn it than have any one read it. Aunt Fanny asked if I was keeping it up. I didn't tell her I forgot to take it along on our trip east. I couldn't have written 1/10th of what happened anyway. Berman said my talk was good.

Sept 22

I sprained my ankle this morning and couldn't go to school. This is tough because I wanted to see Parkie. I keep wondering all day. Ma sure makes a fuss over me and gets me anything I want to eat.

Sept 23

Same as yesterday—pain.

Sept 24

Some better. I'll try to go to school tomorrow. I must see Parkie. I tried to read out of the book I got Sunday but I can't keep my mind on it for wondering. Fred takes my paper route.

Sept 25

Mom didn't want me to very hard, but I went to school anyway. I know now that's Parkie's Pa. Mr. Berman came today to see why I wasn't in Prayer Meeting Wednesday night. It's the first time I've missed since I was baptized. I told him what I heard from Platt's kitchen last Friday night. He said he was shocked beyond measure. He said he may need me later.

Sept 26

Things look mighty serious today. I sometimes wish I hadn't been sitting on the steps just then to hear it, yet how could I help it? I've always wondered how it was to be a detective. Say, Mr. Berman sure knows how to go about anything. Ma is scared terrible the Platt's will be our enemies forever. Pa doesn't say much.

Sept 27

I guess Parkies Pa won't ever forget this day, and neither will I, and I don't suppose Mike and Thad Platt will either. They were arrested for sealing the tires and Parkie's Pa was released. They found a dozen in Platt's cellar. That's what I heard them talking about and laughing over the write up in the newspaper, how Parker had to stand good for it. And to think he bought the two they found on his car from Platt's the night before. He lost his job in the tire shop and besides has to pay Parker the wages he lost while in jail. Parker's going back to his job at the foundry in the morning. I never got mixed up in it all. Mr. Berman saw to that. Ma says she pities Mr. Platt 'cause she's such a nice woman. I'm never, never supposed to tell what I had to do with it. I'll just tell Parkie.

Sept 28

I overslept this morning and had to run to be on time. That man Mr. Berman talked with in the jail last Sunday was there with his wife and the children. The boy was in our class. His name is August Hizen. They took Mr. Berman along home for dinner. They seem just like anybody else and nicer than some. Ma and Pa went over to call on Mrs. Platt. Ma said Mrs. Platt cried most of the time and said that she hoped he'd learn his lesson this time, and we must all pray for another book entitled, "Cutting Through Africa.

Selling Out

By *Christmas Carol Kauffman, age 37, Hannibal, Missouri*
Originally published January 22, 1939,
in the Youth's Christian Companion

The door was unlocked. The mob pressed forward inch by inch. Women gasped for breath; children cried; and various articles were accidentally brushed or knocked off the counters by anxious customers. A red-faced man standing on a table in the center of the store shouted at the top of his voice:

"Come this way, ladies and gentleman. Every article in the store must be sold before Saturday night. Everything goes—wall to wall— at greatly reduced prices. You gain; we lose. Everything in this store is going for less than half price. Anything on this table to my left is selling for one cent. Men's collars, ladies' belts, buttons, shoe strings, thread and dozens of other useful articles for only one cent. We're selling out, ladies and gentleman, wall to wall by Saturday night."

Elizabeth felt a warm hand on her arm and looked up.

"I didn't mean to frighten you."

"You—you didn't," laughed Elizabeth under her breath. The blue belt fell from her hand.

Nancy Lou smiled knowingly, tenderly. "Nice belts for a penny, Elizabeth. If you want it, I'll pay for it."

The young girl looked up at the older one and a puzzled expression crossed her face. "I have a penny," she answered quickly with a frown.

"But let me get it for you anyway. Here is a penny for the blue belt," and she gave the clerk her copper.

"Thank you, Nancy Lou," and Elizabeth tucked the belt into her purse.

"Is there something else on this table you want, Elizabeth? If there is, just say so, and I'll get it for you. Look at this thread for a penny a spool. It certainly is worth that even if some is slightly soiled. I'm going to buy some for my sewing class."

Elizabeth's eyes suddenly opened wide, then fell just as suddenly, and her face got red. She looked away.

"We've been missing you at our meetings." The older girl spoke very softly; for many others were crowded around them. Elizabeth made no answer. "Can't you come next Wednesday evening? We are going to sew for Mrs. Black this time. Can you come, Elizabeth?" Nancy Lou put her arm around the girl and drew her closer to her. A fat man bumped into them and said he was so sorry. "Come with me to the back of the store a minute, Elizabeth."

They went.

"I thought you always enjoyed our sewing class, dear."

"I did."

"I thought you always enjoyed our Sunday-School class too."

"I did."

"I thought you always enjoyed the prayer meetings."

"I did."

"I thought you always enjoyed every activity of the church."

"I did." Elizabeth fumbled with her purse, and her breath came faster and faster. Her lip quivered. Oh, she was pretty!

"Don't you enjoy them anymore, Elizabeth?"

She shook her head.

"Why not?"

"I don't know."

"Shall I make a guess?"

No answer.

"Shall I tell you what I think? Is it my fault?"

She shook her head.

"Is the fault of the class?"

She shook her head.

"Is it the church's fault?"

She shook her head.

"Is it your sister's fault?"

She shook her head.

"Is it your own fault, then?"

Pause. "I guess so."

Her eyes fell.

"Elizabeth, you can't afford to do it."

"Do what?"

"To sell out."

The pretty girl looked up in surprise. She bit her lip.

"That's just what you are doing, my girl, selling out at a greatly reduced price!"

Elizabeth gave a deep sigh.

"Selling your Lord, and your Blessed Savior," Nancy Lou, continued softly, "and your wonderful Christian experience for—for less than half price. Why, Elizabeth!" and the arm around the girl tightened affectionately. "You are exchanging the Lord for—for—you know, Elizabeth. I need not say it. Is it right?"

She shook her head, slowly, very slowly.

"These people here are selling out because the owner has died. They are selling out at any cost. Elizabeth has your owner—"

"No! No!" Her eyes filled with tears. She stiffened her back.

"Those are hard words perhaps; but that's just exactly what many people are doing. Selling out for less—less than a—blue belt, Elizabeth; because their love had died out. Won't you give up the thing that's dragging you away from us, and God, Elizabeth?"

"I'll think about it."

"God bless you, dear. We're praying for you. Remember what Elsie did. Sold out for what?"

"Just a little fun with Ed."

"And where is she today?"

No answer was necessary. Elizabeth looked Nancy Lou straight in the eyes. A great unspeakable longing, mingled with terror reflected from those deep blue windows of her soul. "Oh, if one could only understand the conflict in a girl's soul! A soul, like Elizabeth Ann Walker's."

At the door of the store, Nancy Lou's step got suddenly lighter, when Elizabeth looked up and said smilingly, "I think I'll tell Mack I can't afford to sell out."

Forgive Me

By *Christmas Carol Kauffman, age 37, Hannibal, Missouri*
Originally published June 23, 1939,
in the Youth's Christian Companion

There were eight children in the Ben Sidney family, and Mother Sidney often told folks no two of them were alike, except that they all had hearty appetites, and that they said she was the best cook in all the world.

Old Mose Tomkins, in complimenting Mother Sidney one time on the good behavior of her large family, asked her what method of punishment she used. "Brother Mose," she replied softly with a sacred sweetness on her face, "I have as many methods as children. Little Vivian, I made her sit on the step stool without even a doll to hold in her hand, and Jamie, he must go to a dark closet, and Josephine must miss a meal. Mary can't go to Lucy's house for a week when she has been bad, and Larry—he—he gets the strap. But Amy, bless her heart, the hardest punishment she can get is to kneel down beside Father and pray about it." Mother Sidney's eyes got misty and she looked away.

"How about Flossie?" asked Brother Mose stroking his chin. "And there's Tommy, too, and—"

"That's all of them," she spoke quickly. "Well, Tommy—he needs nothing more severe than a talking to from Father. That's all; but Flossie, she's different somehow. She's caused me more concern than all the rest put together. That's so, Brother Mose. She's so quick tempered and outspoken; it grieves me often. You pray for all of us, especially Flossie."

"I will, Sister,"

And Mother Sidney knew he would do as he promised. He had been like an uncle to the Sidney children since they moved into the community, and they all loved him dearly.

Uncle Mose had a most astonishing grip on God. When he prayed those who heard him knew he was getting straight through to the throne, and they could see the answers he received, too. When Mose prayed in his own secret closet and no one heard, they still knew his prayers were accomplishing great things because he was a righteous man.

The second week in July, Uncle Mose and his good wife, Salome, would be married fifty years, and the Sidney's decided among themselves to have a surprise in their honor. Father Sidney first thought of it and immediately every Sidney down to little Vivian thought it was about the grandest thing Father ever thought of yet. Uncle Mose and his wife would come over for supper, and exactly at eight o'clock, everybody in the church should come marching in and form a circle around the spacious living room, and Mother Sidney would lead out in several familiar hymns suitable for the occasion, and Brother Smith would give some appropriate comments and lead in prayer and several lay members would give short talks, and there would be more music, and before the program ended the Sidney children would sing Uncle Mose's favorite song: "Sitting at the Feet of Jesus." What a happy, happy time the family had talking about it around the supper table. And of course there would be ice cream and cake, and a five dollar gold piece to be presented to Uncle Mose and his wife to get something they needed most.

The members of the church were secretly notified, and everyone seemed anxious to come. A number of the brethren put twice as much toward the gold piece as was suggested, and soon Father Sidney announced to his family that there would be enough to present two five-dollar gold pieces. Little Vivian clapped her hands in delight. "I wish I could be the one to carry it over to them," and her blue eyes sparkled.

"We'll see," said Father.

Saturday afternoon Flossie was cutting out a new dress she wanted to make for the occasion soon to take place. Mother and Father gave the material to her for her birthday some weeks previous. Flossie really did need the new dress. Since she was the oldest of the girls, she could not wear the hand-me-downs. Mary and Amy often thought it would be lovely to be the oldest girl in the family. Dear little Vivian seldom ever got a dress that was what you could call absolutely new out of the store.

Vivian hovered over the table like a little fat bird watching Flossie cut out her new dress. It was so pretty and pink, just like wintergreen candy. "Why, Flossie," she said, "it even smells new, doesn't it?" She held a little scrap of it to her nose and drew a long breath.

At that moment, Amy, who was just eighteen months younger than Flossie, came downstairs with the stepstool in one arm and a pail in the other. Larry and Jamie were having a little fun just around the corner and did not hear Amy coming. They both plunged right into her. Instead of falling she bumped into Flossie, for the table stood about two feet from the stair door. Now Flossie's scissors were sharp, and she was cutting out the back of the waist of the dress.

"Oh, Amy!" she screamed, turning on her sister furiously. "Just look what you made me do, you awkward thing!"

Amy saw the long cut in the back piece of Flossie's new dress. With tears in her eyes, she said, "I'm sorry, Flossie. Oh, I'm so, so sorry! I didn't mean—"

"Yes, you did! Why couldn't you see what I was doing?" retorted Flossie. She was cross.

Little Vivian trembled because she felt sorry for Amy, and because of the cut. She didn't know which to feel sorriest about.

"Well, the boys bumped into me, Flossie," she answered pitifully.

"You just don't want me to have a new dress, you selfish—"

"Oh, Flossie," Amy put down the step stool and pail she had been using in washing windows and, throwing her arms around Flossie, she cried as if her heart would break, "forgive me, please, please, please. I didn't mean to, I didn't, I didn't!"

"My dress is ruined." Flossie shook herself away from Amy. "You are just jealous and don't want me to have a new dress."

"I'm not jealous, Flossie," sobbed Amy, "and I'm sorry. Why won't you believe me and forgive me?" Amy gathered up her pail and step stool and walked away still sobbing.

"Flossie," whispered Vivian gently. "Flossie," she repeated a little louder, "please forgive her." Tears were in her eyes.

Flossie rolled up the dress and went upstairs.

Mother and Father Sydney were working in the garden. "What's that?" Mother's head went up. "Sounds like someone crying in the woodshed." Fathers head went up. "Go see," said Mother.

"Amy, dear, what's the matter?" Father had his arm around her. "What's wrong, Amy? Tell me. You must. What is it, Child?"

"Flossie—Flossie," she choked, "won't—forgive me." Brokenly she told the story.

"Well, well," Father's voice was very low. He kissed Amy tenderly and returned to the garden where Mother was wondering and wondering. She still wondered after Father gave his report.

Amy did not get up the next morning. She had a fever and pain in her right side. Little Vivian stroked her forehead and kissed her hands. Father prayed for her in family worship. At nine o'clock the doctor came and said Amy was a very sick girl and may have to go to the hospital. Little Vivian cried and so did Mary. Tommy and Larry looked sad. They all got ready to go to Sunday school except Mother; yet they did dislike to leave. No one in the family had ever had to go to the hospital, yet. By nine thirty Amy was worse and decidedly so.

"I don't believe I'll go," said Father, and Mother looked somewhat relieved. "You children all go on to Sunday school as usual," he spoke softly in the dining room. "Tell Uncle Mose to come over right away."

Reluctantly the children filed out of the house and down the street. Flossie was the last to leave. Little Vivian took hold of her hand. "Don't you pity Amy, Flossie?" her lips trembled as she looked up.

Flossie nodded. For some reason she could not speak. When they got to the door of the church Flossie whispered to Mary, "You look after Vivian; I'm going back home."

"Going back? Why?"

"'Cause I am."

Mother and Father Sidney were kneeling beside Amy's bed when Flossie stood in the doorway. No one heard her enter. They were praying. She caught her breath for Mother was saying, "Oh dear Lord, help Flossie to forgive and create a new heart within her."

"Amy," she sobbed. There stood Flossie at the foot of the bed; all three jumped. "I'm sorry I treated—treated you so, Amy. I'm sorry. Please forgive me. I know—you didn't—didn't mean to do it," she cried.

"That's alright, Flossie," Amy smiled in spite of her pain. "I forgive you. I hate it that I was so—awkward, but I really didn't mean—"

"I know you didn't. Amy. I was unkind, and—"

In stepped Uncle Mose. He placed a warm hand on Flossie's shoulder and said, "Child, God moves in mysterious ways, His wonders to perform; doesn't He, Flossie?" He had heard only the last four words, but he knew God had heard and answered prayer. Such scenes do not just happen so.

Four of them knelt around Amy's bed and prayed.

"Sh—"whispered Mother when the children arrived. "Be as quiet as possible. Amy is sleeping so nicely."

"And—and won't she have to go to that dreadful hospital, Mother?" asked Vivian and Josephine and Jamie all at the same time.

"It doesn't look like it now," smiled Mother sweetly.

"And do you suppose we can have—have that surprise here on Friday night?" asked Tommy eager faced.

"Well, prayer can do wonders," was Mother Sidney's quick reply.

Marcia Kauffman Clark is the youngest of Nelson Edward and Christmas Carol Kauffman's four children. She moved with her parents and brother James Milton, to Elkhart, Indiana in August 1956. Marcia sang in a sextet with the same six girls all four years while attending Bethany Christian High School in Goshen, Indiana. She attended Hesston College in Hesston Kansas for two years and graduated with a Secondary Education Degree in Home Economics in 1965 from Goshen College, Goshen, Indiana. The greatest highlight of her high school and college years was singing and especially with the traveling choirs while in college. Marcia moved to Phoenix, Arizona, in 1969. She has enjoyed teaching, singing, sewing, and creative writing. She sang first alto in a ladies quartette for twenty-one years. She had the opportunity of traveling in Europe twice as a ten-year member of the Sonoran Desert Chorale. She and her husband, Stephen, live in Tempe, Arizona, and have eight children, twenty-two grandchildren, and one great-grandson.

Marcia Kauffman Clark can be reached by mail at:

1026 East Alameda Drive

Tempe, Arizona 85282

www.ingramcontent.com/pod-product-compliance
Lightning Source LLC
Chambersburg PA
CBHW051127260626
47170CB00005B/1697